LOVE'S
HEALING
POWER

LOVE'S
HEALING
POWER

•

Terry Zahniser
McDermid

AVALON BOOKS
NEW YORK

PRINTED IN THE UNITED STATES OF AMERICA
ON ACID-FREE PAPER
BY HADDON CRAFTSMEN, BLOOMSBURG, PENNSYLVANIA

To good friends and my family,
who remind me daily how important love is.

Chapter One

Amanda Blake pedaled past the car dealership and then braked to a stop. Hopping off her bike, she pulled it over the curb and leaned it against the building. She slipped the lock around the front tire and attached it to a pole before going inside.

The red sports car gleamed in the early morning sun. Sparkling windows displayed the sleek two-seater's interior. She bent down and cupped her hands around her eyes to see the interior better.

"A beauty, isn't she?"

The deep voice startled her, and she straightened up quickly, bumping her head on a small piece of metal protruding from the roof of the car. She rubbed the spot and squinted at the slight pain.

"Sorry. I didn't mean to surprise you." The man moved forward, his fingers pressing gently against her forehead.

1

He massaged her temple for a moment, and the pain seemed to miraculously disappear.

Amanda tilted her head back and looked up at him in surprise. He gave her a lopsided grin and took one step backward. She wiggled her head a few times, but nothing hurt.

"Amazing. A car salesman with magic hands. You've missed your calling. You should be a doctor."

A slight flush rose in his cheeks and his grin disappeared. He dipped his head down; a lock of dark hair dropped over his forehead and shadowed his eyes from her view. "You're interested in this model?" he asked with a gruff tone.

"Well, not really. That is, I pass here every day on the way to work, and today I couldn't resist checking it out."

She followed him around the back of the car. At the passenger side she paused and glanced at the paper attached to the window that listed the many features of the car. The figure at the bottom caught her eye, and she whistled.

He faced her again, one dark eyebrow lifted in question. She pointed to the sticker price of the vehicle. "If I stopped eating for at least three days each week, I could probably afford one of the monthly payments."

His laugh was deep and rich, a sound that brought a smile to her lips and those of a couple standing near the front door. His eyes, a smooth brown that repeated the soft hues of his hair, twinkled.

"Isn't this where you're supposed to convince me that not eating would be good for me?" she asked when he didn't say anything. "That every time I slip under the steering wheel, I'll totally forget that I'm starving."

"First, I would never presume to tell a woman she could get by without eating. She could take it the wrong way. Second, I'm not sure this is the car for you."

Amanda's eyes opened wide. "Not the car for me?" She swung her head around, surveying the rest of the room. A turquoise sedan and a cream luxury car sat on the opposite side. "You surely don't think you'd have more luck trying to sell me one of those?"

He shook his head. "No, actually, I don't think we have the type of car that would best suit you." He tipped his head to one side, studying her carefully. "An all-purpose vehicle, maybe some sort of truck or even a minivan, I would guess."

She bristled a little bit. "A van? Like someone's mother?"

He chuckled. "Maybe I should have tried the not-eating bit. I seem to be making a bigger mess in this direction."

"No, never mind." She waved her hand toward him in a dismissive gesture and headed for the front door. "I've wasted enough time already on this daydream. I just thought this would be a fun way to start my day, before the grind of the salt mill."

His long strides brought him up next to her quickly. "I'm sorry." His lopsided grin again. "I seem to keep apologizing to you."

"It's all right." She touched the handle of the door. "You've brought me back to reality and reminded me I have a job waiting for me."

"Listen." His hand reached out and touched hers, a brief contact that nevertheless stilled her actions and brought her eyes to his in a quick motion. He smiled, his eyes crinkling at the edges, and she caught her breath. "Let me make it up to you," he said. "There's a little diner about a block away. If I can't give you back your daydream, I can at least buy you lunch."

"I don't know." The suddenness of his invitation surprised her, and yet she couldn't stop a small thrill of anticipation at the thought of seeing him again. A warm glow still radiated from the spot where his fingers had touched her skin.

"My name's Doug McCallister. I can get away by 1:00, if that's not too late for you."

She shook her head. "I don't know," she repeated.

"This would be a great way to start saving for the car," he added persuasively. "If I pay for your lunch, you can start saving right away and not have to starve."

A laugh bubbled out of her at his pleading voice and eager look. "Okay, you've convinced me." She shook her head. "I can't believe this. I stop in here on a whim, lose my dream of a car and have a luncheon date. Who's going to believe this?"

He held the door open for her and leaned against it while she unlocked her bike. "Nobody has to believe it," he said. "You just need to be there at 1:00."

She swung her leg over the bike and tucked her curls under the bike helmet. "Or my trusty steed will turn into a pumpkin?" she countered, tapping the handlebars with her free hand.

"Who knows?"

He didn't move, and she pushed off with one foot. She bumped over the curb and slid into the stream of traffic, aware of him still standing in the doorway watching her.

The ride to her office building passed in a blur. *Lunch at the diner,* she thought, weaving through the parked cars to the front door. *With a stranger. At least he's cute.*

She lifted her bike over the curb and balanced it between her legs while she removed her helmet. *Cute doesn't begin to describe him,* she told herself. *With a smile like that, he probably sells a car a minute. And those eyes. You could drown in them and forget your own name.*

The latch on her helmet stuck, and she gave her attention to the two ends for several minutes, wiggling them before they went back together and she could string it over the handlebars. *So why didn't he try to sell me a car?* she thought. *He did everything he could to convince me* not *to buy.*

Her eyebrows drawn together in thought, she pushed the button that opened the front door and slid her bike inside. The security guard lifted his head from his magazine and smiled at her.

"Good morning, Miss Blake."

"Hi, Ronald. Your daughter feeling better?"

He nodded. "She went back to school today. She could hardly wait for the car to stop."

"That's great." Amanda poked the up button for the elevator. When the doors whooshed open, she pushed her bicycle inside. "See you later."

Ronald tipped his head just as the doors closed. She leaned against the back of the elevator, watching the numbers go by. When the doors opened at the sixth floor, she didn't move for a moment and then darted toward the exit when the doors started to slide closed.

Breathing heavily, she tugged her bike down the hall and into a corner office. A trim redhead at the receptionist desk raised her head at Amanda's entrance. "Hi. You're late to-day."

"Thank you, Megan, for that warm greeting." Amanda leaned the bike against the desk and pushed open another door, holding it with her foot and maneuvering the bike into the narrow hallway. "Do I have to beat the rest of you to the office every day?"

Megan grinned. "No, but you do have the rest of them wondering what's going on. Bob thought he should call the police out and have them scour your usual route."

"He couldn't look for me himself?"

"And leave the hallowed grounds in the middle of a pro-ject?" Megan's face portrayed her shock and then relaxed into a smile. "He's waiting in your office. I think he's try-ing to communicate with your aura."

Amanda groaned. "Thank you for the warning." Amanda tucked the bicycle in a shadowed corner of the hallway and smoothed down her jacket and slacks. "Wish me luck."

When she pushed open her office door, the older man sitting near the window didn't move. Morning sun glistened on his full head of white hair. His eyes closed, he raised his hands slowly from his hips and moved them toward his head. He spread his fingers wide, inhaled deeply, and then lowered his hands again.

"Meditating on my whereabouts, Bob?" Amanda tossed her backpack on the floor next to the walnut partner desk covered with papers.

Bob's eyes flicked open, and he dropped his hands before he jumped up. He raced forward and grabbed Amanda's hands. "You're all right!"

She released her hands, stepped around the desk, and plopped into the oversized chair. "I'm fine, Bob. I come to work thirty minutes late, and you have me laid out in the morgue. Bob, we don't live in the big city. Coppertown is lucky to boast 20,000."

"I know, I know." He sat back down and leaned toward her, his hands clasped between his legs. "Amanda, I could sense that you were in trouble. It wasn't very clear, but something was affecting your usual routine."

Amanda opened her mouth with a pithy comment, and the car salesman flashed into her mind. His grin tugged at her insides, and she found it difficult to breathe. A tingle spread from her stomach up through her shoulders and stopped at the spot that he had massaged so gently. Barely aware of her actions, she reached her hand up and brushed it against her temple.

"There it is again!" Bob jumped to his feet. "Amanda, what happened? There's a haze all around you, like you're caught in some sort of force. . . ."

"That's enough, Bob." She had to get control of the situation.

Bob hesitated and then sank back into his seat. "It's still there," he muttered, but he didn't offer any more.

She scooped up a pile of papers. "Okay, let's see where we are on the community center. Sierra and Mark are supposed to come by around 10:00 with some ideas for the ad campaign. We can have Megan draw up a tentative mailing list, and then we need to discuss our plans for the school board meeting. They've said we could have a few minutes on their agenda to introduce the proposal to them and see how the schools can help."

"I thought we could go over to city hall about 1:00," Bob added, scratching notes on the voluminous tablet he always carried with him.

Amanda lifted her head. "1:00? I can't go at 1:00. I have a . . . a," she stopped, uncertain what she had with Doug. "A meeting," she finally said.

"A meeting? But Megan checked your book for me. She said you were free."

"I was yesterday." Amanda was her brisk self again. "Now I'm not." She smiled at Bob. "You can handle it yourself. Or take Megan with you. She can lock up and let the answering service take care of our phone messages."

Bob opened and shut his mouth several times, but no words came out. Amanda waited. She knew he wanted to say something, but since she was his boss, he would be worried about offending her. He finally bit his lower lip and then started to list the people he had contacted. "The doctors at the hospital sounded interested in helping, especially the pediatricians. If we can get a few of the civic groups to sponsor an ad, that would help with the budget."

An hour later, he left the room. Amanda picked up her phone and dialed Megan's exchange. "Any messages come through while we were talking?"

"No. Bob just said you have a lunch meeting at 1:00. It's not in my book."

Darn that nosy Bob. Probably trying to find out what Megan knew. He and that stupid aura business.

Amanda tried to stay calm. "It's not really business, Megan. Just lunch with a friend."

"Okay. Well, I'll be glad to go with Bob and—" her voice lowered—"hold his hand."

Amanda chuckled. "Megan, you shouldn't tease the poor man. He does good work, and his instincts are good."

"Don't let him hear you say that," Megan said. "He's sure it's his aura talking to him."

By the time 12:45 came around, Amanda relished the thought of escaping the tiny office. Sierra and Mark, a husband-and-wife team she had met through a mutual friend when they were down on their luck, flashed idea after idea at her, their words rippling off their tongues in rapid-fire action. Amanda's head swung from one to the other as they shared their ideas, each one adding a word to the other's information. When they walked out of her office, she dropped her head on her desk and moaned.

"I knew it, I knew it!" Bob rushed into the room and rested his hand on her head. "You've had a traumatic experience, and it's just now affecting you."

"Bob, go away." Her hair muffled her words.

"Amanda, I know this is probably difficult for you to talk about right now. You've always been the strong one. . . ."

"Go away right now!" she interrupted.

His voice trailed away. She listened for the sound of her door closing but nothing came. Peeking through the curtain of her hair, she could see Bob standing next to her desk, his green eyes puppy-dog sad.

She sighed and sat up. "I'm sorry, Bob. I shouldn't snap at you like that." He sniffed, and she sighed again. She would have to give him something, or he would never leave her alone. "Listen, Bob, I just stopped at the car dealership on the way to work today. Nothing else happened."

"A car dealership?" She could see his visions of alien abductions disappearing in a trail of diesel fuel.

"A car dealership. The one on the corner, with the fancy sports car. I just thought I'd indulge myself for a minute and not rush to work."

He nodded. "A change, that's what I see. Even though the change may seem minor to you, you're considering a total overhaul of your current lifestyle." He closed his eyes and tilted his head toward the ceiling. "The thought of exchanging your current mode of transportation for one you have consistently fought against is causing you internal strife because of your belief structure."

She pressed her fingertips against her temples. If he didn't have such creative ideas . . . She stopped the thought. He was a sweetheart, and he did have her best interests at heart.

"Bob, you're right." She stood up and ushered him out of the room. "I don't know why I ever try to hide my thoughts from you. My life is on the cusp of a major life change."

"I knew it, I knew it." His craggy face lit in a grin, and she wondered if she had done the right thing. "I can tell right now, Amanda, you're going to be very happy." He frowned and his hands passed over her head. "It's not going to be easy, though."

She patted his shoulder. "Change never is, Bob. Now why don't you find Megan and go over your notes for the meeting at city hall? I need to make a few phone calls before I leave."

He nodded and scurried down the hallway, his tablet under his arm. She took a deep breath and closed the door.

Leaning against it, she thought about Bob's prophecies. The rest of the office staff chuckled at his many pronouncements, but he did have an uncanny ability to find the truth. Could he really have seen something in her encounter with the car salesman that morning?

You're becoming as nutty as Bob, she scolded herself. She grabbed her backpack from the floor. *Just go to lunch and then you can forget all about Doug McCallister.* But even the concentration needed as she joined the throng of lunchtime traffic couldn't dislodge Bob's warning of a coming change.

Chapter Two

Amanda parked her bike near the door and entered the tiny diner. Doug waved at her from a booth near the kitchen. She slid into the seat across from him.

"Hi." He smiled and handed her a menu. "I wasn't sure you would come."

"I wasn't sure myself," she confessed. She fumbled with the menu, aware of the warm look in his eyes, and carefully studied the array of items listed in neat columns.

"The waitress said today's soup was vegetable chicken with rice, and the special had something made from turnips in it."

Amanda lifted her head. "Did you say turnips? I didn't know they served anything with turnips."

He grinned. "You *are* listening to me."

"What are you talking about?"

He shrugged out of his suit coat and the light shirt he wore tightened across his chest. She swallowed and focused on his words. "I was trying to get your attention. I'd much rather see your face than the back of the menu, and you've been ignoring everything else I said. I thought turnips might catch your attention."

She closed the menu and placed it on top of his. "You have my undivided attention now," she said. She didn't want to think about why it was so difficult to concentrate with him sitting across from her. "I would recommend any of their cold sandwiches or salads," she added in a soft voice, after a quick glance to be sure the waitress was out of range. "I've never been too sure of their cooking arrangements here."

"Thanks for the warning. I usually go home for lunch, but several of the other salesmen eat here every day."

"Home?" A little pang settled in the middle of her stomach. "You don't mean home like with a wife and family, do you?"

A long pause filled the space around them. "No," he finally said without looking at her. "I'm not married."

"Not that I would mind," she added quickly. "It's just that I'm working on a tricky account right now and our opponents would love to find anything they could use against us." *And discovering that I met a married man for lunch would be great fodder for their arguments,* she thought.

He leaned against the back of the plastic-coated seat and rested one arm along the top of it. "What do you do? I realized after you left this morning that I don't know anything about you. Not even your name."

She sipped her water before answering. She already regretted the impulse that had brought her to the diner. Her busy schedule left her little time for socializing, and her body's response to the possibility that he might be married had annoyed her. She didn't need a man complicating her life right now.

He smiled at her, and she swallowed her water. She was here with him now, and nothing would change that. She would just be polite, carry on a surface conversation and make her escape as soon as possible. Then she would put Doug McCallister out of her mind and concentrate on her work. "Amanda Blake. I run a small advertising agency here in town."

"Oh." He seemed to consider this for a moment. "So I probably insulted you this morning when I said you didn't look like the type for a sports car."

"Well, you did surprise me," she conceded. "I thought you would try to convince me to at least take a test-drive. But you were right. I can't afford it. Starting my own business has taken every last dime I had saved up and some more besides."

The waitress stopped by their booth, and the conversation shifted to their orders. After the woman wrote down two tossed salads and roast beef sandwiches, she tucked her pencil into her apron pocket and disappeared into the kitchen. Doug leaned his elbows on the table. "What do you advertise?"

"None of the major products you see on television or in magazines," she said. "I started the agency to help advertise and promote community projects. We also work with companies that want to improve their image in the community."

He nodded. "What are you working on right now?"

"Are you sure you want to hear all this?" She watched him carefully, trying to see if he was truly interested or only making polite conversation.

"Yes."

The glint in his eyes convinced her more than his single word. "Several small accounts, television spots, newspaper ads, community awareness, that sort of thing. The major project, though, is a joint effort with several of the civic groups to renovate a community building."

"Doesn't the town have a community building? I remember meeting with some sort of professional group in an old building at the edge of town a few years ago."

"Probably Parker Hall." She tucked several curls behind her ear and leaned toward him. "The civic groups in town meet in several old buildings like that. A few were fire stations at the turn of the century that weren't needed when the new stations were built. One group meets in a drafty, one-room building that used to be the town livery."

"So why the sudden urge for a community building?"

Amanda accepted her plate of food from the waitress with a soft thank you. "We're not building a new one. A descendant of one of the founding fathers died last summer and left her house to the city. You've probably seen it. The Willowton House?" He nodded. "An architect in town offered to draw up renovation plans for free, and most of the materials have already been donated by building suppliers."

"Where do you come in? It sounds like it's a done deal."

She pressed her lips together and nodded. "Should be. Unfortunately a small group of people are opposed to the idea of a community center. They want the city to tear down the building and make a park instead."

Doug lifted the top piece of bread and added lettuce and tomato to his sandwich. "The other parks aren't enough?"

"I guess not. My own feeling is that they brought up the park just to stop the community building." Amanda shifted her plate away from the edge of the table, too caught up in the conversation to eat. "How can you argue against a park? It sounds like you're arguing against children. But a community building would give the children and others in the city a place to go during the winter and bad weather. For a city this size, we could put a building like that to use every day and night of the year."

Doug ran his hand through his hair, and the unruly lock fell forward again. "And your job is to convince the community that they want the building?"

She nodded. "We should be spending our energy on renovating the building, and organizing staff and programs. Instead, we're campaigning for votes. The opposition is very vocal. They've been writing letters to the editors stating that a community building would lead to children being unsupervised and reminding the city leaders that parents should decide how their children spend their time."

"So that's why you wanted to know if I was married. If they found out you were seeing a married man, they'd use the information to support their arguments."

Amanda grinned at his quick assessment. "Exactly. They're looking for anything they can use to show that the center would lead the children astray."

"Instead of focusing on the fact that a center like that would be good for the community and would provide, not only the children, but seniors, families and business people a place to gather. A return to the central meeting place that used to exist in most towns."

Amanda tipped her head to one side. "You wouldn't be interested in helping on our side, would you? We need people to talk to the different groups in town, and you sound like a great campaigner."

"No, thanks." He smiled at her, softening his refusal. "I wouldn't mind helping, but I'd prefer to stay behind the scenes."

"That's okay." She pushed a piece of lettuce around her plate. While she listened to his comments about the community center, an idea had begun to form in her mind. She wondered if she was crazy to even consider the next step.

When the words came out of her mouth, she felt as if she had stepped away from the worn-out booth and was watching a scene in a play. "You wouldn't want to come to dinner with my family tomorrow night, would you?"

He didn't answer right away. *Maybe I didn't really say it out loud,* she thought. *Maybe I just imagined I asked him.*

But his answer removed all doubt. "Any special reason you want me to meet your family?"

In for a penny, in for a pound. "My brother just got engaged, and we're celebrating tomorrow night with a family dinner. My two sisters will be there with their husbands, and now my brother's bringing the love of his life."

"And it would help if you had a date yourself."

She nodded. Again he had cut straight to the heart of the problem. "I could mention that we met during my work on the community center account. They wouldn't need to know anything else about our relationship."

"What would happen if you went by yourself?"

Amanda bit her lower lip and studied a stain on the tablecloth. "My parents can't understand why I'm not married yet. Not that they think marriage is the only career for women . . ." She trailed off, uncertain how to explain her parents' point of view to him.

"I take it your parents are happily married?"

She raised her head and smiled at him. "Very. In fact, my sisters and I used to wonder if our parents even knew we were around. They always seemed to be wrapped up in each other."

He collected the bill from the waitress and waited while Amanda crawled out of the narrow seat. His hand lightly touched her back on the way to the cash register, and she liked the gentle feel of his fingers. A tiny tingle settled in her lower spine and radiated toward the rest of her body.

"It sounds like you were lucky," he said once they were outside. He removed his hand from her back and pressed both of them into his pockets. She stopped near her bike. "Not everyone has a good example of a loving relationship. They probably want you to have the same experience."

"I know. It's just that sometimes . . ." She hesitated, unsure how to voice her feelings, or why she felt it was so important to share them with this man she had just met. "Sometimes I just don't think I'm cut out for that kind of life."

"Marriage?"

"A husband, kids, cooking, cleaning, carpools, grocery shopping, laundry." She ticked off each item on her fingers. "Even my friends who have full-time careers still spend a lot of time at home with the housework."

"Marriage is more than a list of chores."

She bent down and unlocked her bike, wrapping the lock around the bar under her seat. "Maybe. But it just seems to me that the man gets the major benefits when it comes to a marriage. I have a good job, my own house, and I don't have to please anyone but myself. Why should I change?"

He grasped her handlebars and held the bike while she climbed on. "There is more to marriage," he said softly.

His breath tickled her cheek, and she could feel moisture on her palms as they gripped the handlebars. She couldn't drag her eyes away from his steady gaze. Her heart pounded against her chest, and when he stood up, she felt as if she had already ridden her bike several hard miles.

He moved away from the bike and crossed his arms over his chest. "So are you warning me that tomorrow will strictly be a play-acting situation? What will happen when they find out we aren't seeing each other again?"

"I don't think they'll be surprised," she said slowly.

His eyes narrowed. "I see. A car salesman isn't exactly the perfect mate for an independent businesswoman."

"That's not what I mean at all." She reached a hand toward him and clasped his arm just below the elbow. Firm muscles rippled under her fingers. "My parents would never say anything about any of my dates. And if you're happy in your choice of career, then that's great."

"Then what?"

She took a deep breath. She didn't like admitting this character flaw to herself, let alone to this man she had just met. But she owed him at least this much if he would agree to the masquerade. "I'm not known for being the best judge of character when it comes to the men I date. Most of them don't hang around after a visit with my family."

"They don't pass the test? And since I'm a car sales-man . . ." One corner of his mouth started to raise in his lazy grin.

"I have nothing against your career choice," she snapped. "You're the one who keeps bringing it up. And since you do, you have to admit your profession isn't known for be-ing the most honest in business. Those surveys they do of careers always put people who sell cars near the bottom of the trust level."

"I guess I deserve that." His smile broadened. "But now I feel like I have to go, if only in defense of all my fellow car dealers."

"Then you'll come?" She waited anxiously for his an-swer. She hadn't realized how much she was counting on him to help her deal with her mother's gushing excitement over Tim's engagement.

"I'll come. What time should I pick you up, and where?"

Relief flooded her at his acceptance. "Oh, you don't have to pick me up. We can just meet at my parents' house."

His smile disappeared. "I can pick up my date."

"But it's not really a date, Doug." She had to assert her-self and keep a distance. This man already had gathered facts about her no one else knew. She didn't know why, but she had a niggling fear that once she let him into her small house, she'd never be able to call her soul her own again.

"I don't live that far from them," she explained, giving him the address. "This way, if you want to leave early, you won't feel obligated to see me home."

"I won't run out on you. What time should I be there?"

"Around 7:00 will be fine." She had this compelling urge to keep touching him, and she rested her fingers against the soft cotton of his long-sleeved shirt. "And thank you. I really appreciate this."

"You're welcome," he muttered. "Now I suppose I should get back to the dealership. You probably have work to do, too."

She glanced at her watch. 3:00. "Oh, my goodness. I've never taken a two-hour lunch before. I just hope Bob's not back, or he'll be combing the hospitals."

"Bob?"

She pushed on the pedals and bounced over the curb. "I'll explain tomorrow," she called over her shoulder and threaded her way through the traffic.

The office door was still locked when she arrived. She turned on the lights and leaned her bike in its customary position before hurrying into her office. She had just pulled out a folder when she heard the knob turn on the outer office door. With a sigh of relief, she bent over the pages and tried to look as if she had been studying the words for hours.

"Hi, Amanda, we're back," Bob announced from her doorway.

Amanda lifted her head. "Have a good meeting?"

He nodded and sat down across from her. "If the proposal passes next week, we'll be ready to start the renovations. I think we can go ahead with the plans for the fundraising dance next Friday. Since we're only asking to use the property, and no funds are needed from the voters, we shouldn't have any problem."

"We didn't think we'd have any problem when the proposal was first made." She shuffled through the stack of papers on her desk and picked up several stapled together. "This is the initial report on the building and the necessary repairs. We should be working on this, advertising the possibilities of the center and working on the fundraising campaign, not trying to find votes."

"It will be fine, Amanda." Bob beamed at her. "When we were leaving city hall, I could see roof of the Willowton House, and it had a rosy aura around it. A very positive sign."

Amanda tapped a pencil on her desk. "Bob, I know you mean well, but it's going to take more than auras to make sure the vote passes."

Bob frowned and bent forward, waving his hand in front of her face. She blinked and ducked away from him.

"Something's happened!" he crowed. "You've had another shift in your life. I can feel a positive glow pulsating from your being."

Her chair creaked as she pushed it back and stood up. "Bob, I have work to do, and so do you. The Forsythe account is due this week, and we still have to finalize the television commercials for the library."

Bob scrambled to his feet. "Amanda, I didn't mean to upset you."

She took a deep breath and counted to ten. "You didn't upset me, Bob. I just think we've had enough talk of auras and life changes today. Why don't you meet with Megan and see if any of the actors we used for the science museum would work for the library spots? That should take up the rest of the afternoon."

He nodded and backed toward the door. "Amanda, I just have your best interests at heart."

She sighed. She hated the way his brow puckered when he thought she was upset with him. "I know. I don't mean to be grumpy. I'm just thinking about the work ahead of us. We can't afford to hire anyone else this quarter, which means we have to keep our minds focused on the projects at hand."

"I can work overtime," he offered. "Whatever it takes to help, Amanda."

She walked him to her office door. "I appreciate that, Bob. If you can find the right actors for the library commercials and then see about the Forsythe account, that will be great."

"I will. You can count on me." He scurried out of the door, and she soon heard him asking Megan for a list of actors they had used in the past.

She shut the door and sat back at her desk. She dropped her head on her arms and wondered if Bob could possibly be right. Since meeting Doug, her mind had wandered, she had taken her first two-hour lunch break and twice she had offended one of her most loyal employees.

After her family met Doug, she could go back to her independent lifestyle. Tim's marriage would keep her mother occupied for at least the next few months, and her sisters were busy with their own lives. It might sound cruel, but she only needed Doug around to buy her some breathing space.

Now he was getting in the way. She pushed the thought of Doug and auras out of her mind. The school board wanted to know what the schools could expect from the community building, and she had some preliminary reports to study. She flipped open a folder and forced herself to forget liquid brown eyes and a soft, husky voice that seemed to penetrate every fiber of her being.

Chapter Three

From outside the door of her small house, Amanda could hear the phone ringing. "I'm coming!" she hollered in desperation. She twisted her backpack around and rummaged through the front pocket for her house key.

The answering machine whirred and buzzed as she entered the room. She dropped the backpack on the floor just in time to hear her mother's voice. She hesitated, her hand above the phone.

"Amanda, dear, we'll be eating about 7:30." Her mother's voice floated around the room, echoing through the speaker of the answering machine. "We're so excited about meeting your young man. Why don't you wear that pretty blue dress you wore at Easter? It brings out the blue of your eyes."

Amanda groaned and settled into a chair across from the phone. Her mother continued with several other suggestions about Amanda's attire and then signed off with a smacking sound and a "love you."

She punched the button on her machine. A friend and Bob had both left messages, neither requiring her to do anything but listen. She shuffled through the small stack of mail she had brought into the house and then headed down the short hallway to the bedroom at the end.

A blue dress lay on the bed, a pair of cream pumps on the floor beneath it. She scooped up the dress and stuffed it onto a hanger before placing it back in the closet. With a sigh, she sorted through the few dresses that hung at the end of her closet.

"Great, Mother, now what am I going to do?" she asked the air. "If I wear the blue dress, you'll be sure I was following your directions. But I don't have anything else that looks half as good."

She finally dug a pair of dark blue jeans out of her dresser drawer and jammed her legs into them with a defiant air. Geometric patterns in bright reds, yellows, and blues danced across the front of the sweater she pulled over her head. Her tennis shoes boasted the same bold design.

Standing in front of the mirror, she brushed her curls into a semblance of order and wished for the thousandth time that she had more blonde in her hair than brown. "At least my sweater brings out the blue in my eyes," she said with a giggle.

When she rang the doorbell at her mother's house, she waited for the inevitable gasp and hug. Patricia Blake didn't disappoint her. The deep blue eyes that each of the four children had inherited widened in frustration and then crinkled at the corners as she swept Amanda into a deep hug.

"You look lovely, dear," her mother said, not an ounce of criticism in her voice. Amanda grinned. "Thank you," Amanda said. "I hope I'm not too casual."

"Not at all." Her mother leaned around her and glanced toward the empty doorway. "But where's your young man?"

"Mom, this isn't the twenties." Amanda gently closed the door against the still lingering winter air. "He isn't my young man. He's just someone I met while I was working on an account, and he agreed to come to dinner with me."

Her mother linked her arm through her daughter's. "Well, we're all anxious to meet him. Now, come into the kitchen with me. Jill's already there, and we can visit for a few minutes before the rest of them get here."

In the kitchen, the sister closest to Amanda in age stood at the counter tossing a salad. Amanda paused on the threshold, amazed as always that this gorgeous creature was related to her. Jill's figure was still a perfect size six, even after two children. Her burnished gold hair sparkled under the kitchen light. Smooth creamy cheeks and a rosebud mouth complemented her deep blue eyes. Amanda knew from photo albums that Jill was the image of their mother at the same age.

Jill turned her head and grinned at them. A dimple in her right cheek gave personality to the model-perfect picture she presented. "Hi, Amanda. Did you come early to help cook?"

Amanda stuck out her tongue, and Jill laughed. Their mother clucked at them. "Girls, act your ages."

"I am, Mother," Jill said. She flicked her hair over her shoulder. "Amanda's the one being childish."

"You asked the leading question," Amanda challenged.

A tall, lanky man entered the room. His walk and athletic build showed where Amanda had gotten her figure. He draped an arm around her shoulders.

"Are they picking on you, Peanut?"

"Yes, Daddy." Amanda grinned at her sister from the security of her father's arm. "They think I can't cook."

"Oh, dear. I don't think I want to get in the middle of this one." He dropped his arm and moved around the counter. He grabbed his wife around the middle and lifted her several inches into the air, planting a kiss on her lips before he set her down.

"Now who's acting their ages?" Jill asked.

Stan Blake wagged a finger at his daughter. "You, young lady, can still be sent to your room."

"My wife's going to her room? What's she done now?"

"She's not being very respectful," Patricia told her son-in-law from under the shelter of her husband's arms.

Brent crossed the room in two long strides and wrapped his arms around his wife's waist. She wriggled a moment, protesting that he would spill the salad, and then subsided in his hold, lifting her face for his kiss.

Amanda slipped from the room, embarrassed by the emotions floating around the kitchen. She dearly loved her parents, and both her sisters and their husbands, but sometimes she wondered why they couldn't confine their affectionate displays to their own homes. She picked up a magazine and plopped down on the couch, resting her feet on a hassock her mother had decorated with needlepoint.

A muffled knock roused her from her reading. When she pulled open the door, she found her eldest sister standing on the doormat, a blanketed bundle in her arms.

"Don't say anything," Christine warned. A frown marred a face as lovely as that of Jill's. She came into the room followed by her husband, Scott, and a little boy of four.

"What would I say?"

"I promised Mom I wouldn't bring the boys. But the sitter called fifteen minutes ago and cancelled." Christine handed the small bundle to her husband and shrugged out of her coat.

Amanda took the coats and added them to the pile already stacked on her parents' bed. Fresh gardenias and carnations brought springtime into the room, and she inhaled deeply. Armed against her family's shifting moods, she pushed open the swinging door and joined them in the kitchen.

"I don't know, Mom," Christine was saying. She had unwrapped the baby and was sitting on a kitchen chair bouncing him on her knees. "I really think she decided she'd rather not baby-sit tonight and slipped off to meet some boy."

"Christine, you don't believe that." Her husband handed Aaron a red crayon and ruffled his son's hair. Amanda smiled at them and sat down on a counter stool, wrapping her legs around the bottom rung.

Christine sniffed. "Well, don't you think it's suspicious that she called just before we were ready to go? She's never been very reliable."

"Then why do you keep using her?" Jill carried the finished salad bowl over to the table and sat down across from her sister. "I've told you I have a list of baby-sitters as long as your arm."

The doorbell chimed through the house. Amanda jumped to her feet. "I'll get it."

The swinging door didn't cut off their conversation. "What do you know about her date?" Christine asked.

"Nothing," her mother replied. "She just said he's someone she met while she was working on this new account."

Amanda bowed her head and wondered if she could make a run for it. Knowing they would only find her sooner or later, she took a deep breath and pulled the door open.

Her brother stood on the front porch, locked in a deep embrace with his fiancée. "Hi," Amanda said brightly.

Tim lifted his head but didn't loosen his hold on Jenette. The younger woman gave Amanda a shy smile. "Are we late?"

"No, everyone isn't here yet." Amanda held the door open for them. "The rest of the family is in the kitchen."

She watched Tim lead Jenette into the house. They paused on the edge of the living room for another kiss, and then he pushed open the swinging door. She could hear the shouts of greeting from the rest of the family.

She pulled the door closed and sank down onto the front stoop. The cement bit into her legs and thighs, but she didn't mind the cold. Doug wasn't going to come, and she would have to face the loving concern in her family's eyes. They wouldn't say anything, but she knew they would all be thinking the same thing.

Her family wanted her to be happy, too. They wanted her to find someone who cares.

She pulled her knees into her chest and rested her chin on top of them. A fable from her childhood came to mind.

"The Greeks believed that people used to have two heads and four legs," Jill had told a fascinated younger Amanda. "Then the gods decided to split everyone in half. Soon everyone had only one head and two legs. But they forgot that everyone had only one soul. And so each person is destined to wander the earth, looking for the other half of his or her soul."

"What are you thinking about so hard?"

Amanda jerked and almost fell off the step. Doug's hand wrapped around her arm and held onto her. She pressed her other hand against her chest and inhaled deeply several times.

"Where did you come from?" she asked when she could breathe normally again.

He sat down next to her, his hand still holding onto her. "From the car over there." He pointed to a shiny gray sedan parked at the edge of the sidewalk. Jill and Christine had parked their much older cars in the driveway. "Didn't you hear me drive up?"

Amanda shook her head, glad it was dark outside. Her cheeks felt flushed, and she didn't know if it was because of his touch or her strange thoughts just before his arrival.

"I'm sorry I'm late. I had to close the dealership tonight, and this young couple came into the store right at closing time. They wanted to check out every car in the show-room." His voice sounded tired.

"Did you sell them a car?"

"Not yet. But I'm sure they're going to buy something. Daddy's paying the bill."

"Is that bitterness I hear?"

She could feel him shake his head. "No. Just a little worry. They're awfully young, but they need to learn how to take care of themselves. They won't be able to count on Daddy all the time."

"Some families never get too old to take care of each other." She thought of her father's earlier defense of her in the kitchen.

"I know. And it's not that I think they should have to struggle on their own. I just see too many young couples getting themselves into debt because they've always had everything, and then they don't know how to get out of it."

A giggle burst out of Amanda at his somber words. She clapped a hand over her mouth, but not before Doug had heard it. "You think debt is funny?"

She tried to get herself under control. Ever since he had sat down beside her, she had felt her emotions swirling around inside her. Happiness bubbled up because he hadn't let her down, but she couldn't tell him that. "Of course not, Doug. But you sound so serious. How old are you any-way?"

"I'm thirty-five."

"Well, you sound older than my dad." She stood up and tugged at his hand until he joined her on the step. "Come on. You've had a hard day, and you need some cheering up. My family will do just that."

He hesitated at the door. "Amanda, before we go in, I think I should tell you something."

"What?"

"I haven't been completely honest with you."

She laughed. "I know that. You sell cars, remember?"

"No, it's something else."

The door flew open and bathed them both in the soft light of the entryway. "Here they are, Mom!" Jill called out in her throaty voice. The family materialized behind her, each of them smiling in the direction of the front door.

Jill faced Amanda again. "Mom's been worried about you. She thought you ran off."

"I just went out for some air." Amanda stepped into the warmth of the house, Doug behind her. "Doug was just driving up, so we were talking a minute."

"Oh, good, he's here." Jill reached out a hand toward Doug as he entered the house. "I'm Jill Stone, Amanda's sister."

Doug shook her hand. "Hello, I'm . . ."

"Doctor McCallister!" Jill finished in a rush, her eyes wide with shock.

Amanda glanced from her sister to Doug. His eyes stood out in stark relief, and his mouth was a straight line. He seemed to be struggling with some dark emotion.

"Amanda, you didn't tell us you were bringing Doctor McCallister." Jill smiled at him. "I'm so glad to hear you're back in town. We were so sorry about Mary. I always loved working with her on the hospital projects."

"Thank you," Doug mumbled.

Amanda swung her head between Doug and her sister in confusion. "You know him?"

"He was our pediatrician when Luke and Anna were littler." Jill frowned and caught her full lower lip between perfect white teeth. "You quit practicing, didn't you?"

He nodded. "I just came back to town a few days ago."

Amanda reached behind her until she felt the comforting solidity of a chair. She sank into it and stared at Doug.

"You used to live here before? You were a doctor?" Her mouth felt thick, and the words barely pushed through her lips.

Jill frowned. "Oh, dear, have I said something I shouldn't have? Brent's always complaining that I speak before I think."

"It's all right," Doug assured her. "I should have told Amanda before this."

"Told me what?" Amanda asked.

"I think we'll wait in the kitchen." Jill shooed the rest of the family out of the living room, and Amanda found herself alone with Doug.

Doug perched on the edge of a chair opposite Amanda. She hardly recognized the man she had met the day before. His eyes had lost their brilliance and were a dull mud color. The color had drained from his cheeks, and a dark shadow covered the lower half of his face. He ran his hand through his hair several times, causing the unruly lock to bounce up and down over his forehead.

"Doug, what's the matter?" She whispered the words, afraid of the tension that permeated the room.

"Amanda, I was married before."

Amanda let out her breath in a slow whoosh, unaware until that moment that she had been holding it. "That's all? But a lot of people have been married before."

He nodded. "I know." He closed his eyes but not before Amanda saw the pain in them. When he opened them again, their color had changed to a clear amber and a bleak expression filled them. "Mary died and I couldn't save her."

"Oh, Doug." Amanda reached across the space and cupped his shoulders with her hands, squeezing them gently. "I'm sure you did your best."

He shook his head. "No, I wasn't even there." He sighed, and his body shuddered with the action. "She was running an errand I said I would do." He smashed one clenched fist into the palm of his other hand. "But I didn't get home in time, and she went without me."

"Doug, you can't blame yourself."

Now his eyes sparkled with anger, whether at herself or him, she couldn't tell. "Why not? You weren't there. You don't know what happened."

She recoiled backward at the venom in his voice and dropped her hands into her lap. He lowered his head into his hands and rocked back and forth several times.

The kitchen door moved, and she glanced over his shoulder. Jill's concerned face peeped out, and Amanda shook her head vigorously several times. Her sister disappeared into the kitchen, but Amanda knew she probably had her ear pressed against the wooden door.

Doug lifted his ravaged face. "If you don't mind, I think I'll go home tonight."

"Are you sure you should be alone?"

"I'll be fine, Amanda. I just don't think I'm very good company tonight."

He stood up, and Amanda followed him to the door. He gave her a sad smile. "I told you I wouldn't run out on you, and here I am, leaving before I even meet your parents."

"I don't care about that. I'm worried about you. Will you be okay?"

He caught the edge of her chin with an index finger and tipped her head until their faces were only inches away from each other. "I just need a little more time." His lips brushed lightly against hers. "Will you give me that?"

With her eyes half-closed, she nodded. His kiss had been the slightest of touches, and yet it had awakened a part of her she didn't know existed, some inner core of her being that cried out to him.

"I'll call you." His hand cupped her cheek for a moment, and he gazed into her eyes with a hungry look. Then he yanked open the door and disappeared into the night.

Chapter Four

Amanda waited for several seconds after the muffled sounds of his car faded away before she closed the door. A few moments later, her family joined her in the living room.

"Oh, Amanda, I'm sorry." Jill grabbed her hands and squeezed them tightly.

"It's okay," Amanda said. She sat down in a chair, her mind numbed by the events of the last few minutes.

"But I didn't realize you were bringing Doctor McCallister. If you had warned me, I wouldn't have said anything."

"It's okay," Amanda repeated.

Jill sank down in a graceful heap on the couch. "I didn't even know he was back. It was so sad. Mary was such a sweetheart. And to die like that." She clicked her tongue against the roof of her mouth and shook her head back and forth.

Amanda closed her eyes and took several cleansing breaths. When she opened her eyes again, she found the rest of the family focused on her.

"Amanda, you don't know what Jill's talking about, do you?" Christine asked.

Amanda shook her head. "I didn't know he was a doctor until Jill said something. And Doug just said that he had been married before, and that his wife died."

Jill, Christine, and their mother glanced at one another. Amanda knew they were circling their wagons. For once she was glad of their protective stance.

"We need to tell her," Christine said softly.

Patricia nodded at her daughters. "You girls tell her. You knew his wife the best."

"Amanda, I don't know what your feelings are for Dr. McCallister, but this may hurt," Jill said with an anxious frown.

"I just met him," Amanda said calmly. She couldn't admit her newly awakened feelings in the midst of her family. They were still too raw to identify.

"Well, I think it's important you know about his past."

"Just tell her," Brent said from his corner of the couch. "The build-up is taking longer than the story."

Jill frowned at her husband. "It's just that this might be difficult for Amanda to hear."

Amanda couldn't stand the suspense. "Jill, please," she begged, her calm facade slipping.

"All right. Now you have to remember that I don't know everything. I met Dr. McCallister's wife at a hospital fundraising. Luke was probably three or four, and I was expecting Anna."

Amanda held her body rigid as Jill explained how she had worked with Mary McCallister on several fundraising projects for the hospital. The two women became good friends and spent time at each other's houses.

"She loved to come over to my house," Jill said. "She thought the world of Luke. They wanted to have children, but nothing had happened.

"Then she found out she was pregnant. I remember she came over with a present for Anna. Mary was so happy, she positively glowed. When she picked up Anna and held her for the first time, I knew she was pregnant. When I asked her, she nodded, and her face lit up from within."

Jill paused. Amanda waited, her entire body on edge.

"Then what happened?" she whispered when Jill didn't speak.

"I'm not sure. I visited her at home one day shortly before she died. She'd stopped coming to the meetings of the auxiliary, and I wondered how she was doing." Jill shook her head, her curls bouncing around her shoulders. "She said that she didn't want to do anything that would hurt the baby, and she didn't like the thought of the seatbelt pressing on her stomach. They'd been trying for so many years that she was afraid if something happened to this baby, she'd never have another one.

"She had promised Doug she wouldn't go out in the car because she wouldn't wear her seatbelt. He was adamant that they always wear seatbelts. He did such a good job with his patients that Luke would start screaming if I started the car before he was completely buckled."

The living room crackled with tension as Jill continued. "I still don't know why she left the house. She was about a block from home when a teenager ran a stop sign and hit her car. She was thrown out of the car and died instantly."

Amanda bit back a sob and lowered her head, her heart thudding with pain for the young woman who had nurtured such hopes for her baby and the young doctor who had been her husband. She saw again the pain in Doug's eyes and her soul reached across the distance to share his anguish.

"Doug quit his practice," Jill said quietly. "He said that if he couldn't save his own wife and child, he had no business trying to help anyone else. He left town and until tonight, he just disappeared."

The room was silent. Amanda brushed the tears from her cheeks and lifted her head. Her family watched her quietly.

"Are you all right?" her mother asked.

"A little numb," Amanda admitted. "I didn't know any of this. When did it happen?"

"About five years ago," Christine said. "You were still at college, I guess."

Amanda nodded. "I feel a little confused. I mean, I just met him yesterday and I didn't have a clue about all of this."

"Do you want to lie down?" her mother asked, starting to get to her feet.

"No." She smiled apologetically at her brother. "This was supposed to be a celebration. Now you see why I shouldn't try to date."

"Amanda!" Her mother's eyebrows raised in dismay.

"I'm sorry, Mom. I didn't mean that the way it sounded." She stood up. "Maybe I should just go home."

Her sisters leaped to their feet, each grabbing one of her arms. "Amanda, you don't need to be alone," Christine said.

"At least stay for dinner," Jill added.

"If she wants to go home, let her."

The three sisters turned at the sound of Scott's voice. "But she shouldn't be alone," Christine argued with her husband.

"She doesn't need all of you fussing over her." He detached his wife's hand from Amanda's arm and smiled at his sister-in-law. "Go home and take a warm bath. You'll feel better after a good night's sleep."

Amanda leaned forward and kissed him on the cheek. "Thank you, Scott. I think that's a good idea." She patted Christine on the cheek and then kissed her gently. "You'll all have a better time if I'm not here."

Her mother rushed into the bedroom and returned with Amanda's coat. Tim helped her into it and hugged her tightly. Her sisters and mother both hugged her, patted her on the back, and begged her to call if she needed to talk. Jenette hung back from the crowd at the door, and Amanda made her way to the young woman.

"I'm sorry I ruined your party," she said softly. "I promise to make it up to you later."

"It's all right." Jenette patted Amanda's shoulder. "I hope everything will work out."

"It will," Patricia said in a bright, cheerful voice. She wrapped a hand around Amanda's arm and bundled her toward the door. "Now call me as soon as you get home."

"Mom, I'm only going a few blocks."

"Call me." Her mother's tone left no room for refusal.

Amanda clicked on her bicycle light and pedaled slowly down the streets. A few lights flickered between cracks in the curtains of the homes she passed, and she could see the blue lights of the television sets. Family groups clustered together, and she wondered if she should have stayed at her parents' house.

But their well-meaning concern had been cloying, and she welcomed the crisp night air. A slight breeze ruffled the curls that escaped her helmet. Clouds floated overhead, their dark shadows playing hide-and-seek with the moon.

The peaceful night soothed her spirits. The romantic thoughts she kept hidden from her family came into full play as she cycled down the quiet streets. She had never lost anyone close to her. Was five years enough time to grieve? Did Doug's arrival back in town mean that he was ready for another relationship? Could she be the one to help him recover? Did she want to be?

The questions tumbled over each other. A bird fluttered past her head, and a night creature scurried into the bushes when she rode over the curb and toward the small shed where she parked her bike. Intent on her daydreaming, she crossed the last few steps to her front porch. A soft sound in front of her brought her back to reality, and she gasped when a dark shape stood up.

She stumbled backward before the person grabbed her arm. Her mouth opened, but the scream stuck in her throat as a large hand clamped itself over her mouth. She started to bite it and then heard Doug's low rumble in her ear. "Don't scream, it's me."

He released his hold, and she whirled around, her chest heaving as she caught her breath. "What are you doing, sneaking up on a person like that? I could have had a heart attack."

"Why weren't you paying attention? What if it hadn't been me?"

"Well, it *was* you. You should have said something when you saw me come into the driveway." She plunked her hands on her hips and glared at him.

"I did. I thought you were ignoring me, still upset because I didn't tell you the truth earlier. I was just getting ready to go home."

The enormity of what she had heard earlier drained the rest of her indignation. She sank onto the top stoop and buried her head in her hands. "Oh, Doug, I'm sorry. I'm acting like a fool." She lifted her head, her eyes narrowed. "How did you know where I lived?"

He sat down next to her, his hands resting on his knees. "You're in the phone book, Amanda. I looked it up after I left your parents' house. I didn't want to leave things the way they were."

A warm feeling spread through her insides, wiping away her earlier fear. She shifted around until she could see his face in the dim glow from the streetlight. "I'm sorry about your wife, Doug."

His fingers touched her hand briefly. "Thank you." He gave a little sigh that ruffled the hair above her right ear. "I thought I was ready to come back. After she died, I couldn't settle anywhere, and when my cousin asked me to come work for him, I thought it would help."

And tonight reminded you of everything you lost, Amanda thought. A tear slid under her lashes and trickled down her cheek. "Do you want to talk about it?" she asked softly.

"I wouldn't know where to start. Mary was part of my life for a good many years. She helped me through medical school and stuck with me when times were really lean. When I accepted the position here, we thought we were settled for life. Then she had the car accident, and I didn't know what I wanted to do."

"Why did you quit practicing?"

The silence wrapped around her, deep, penetrating, filled with guilt and anger, and other emotions she couldn't identify.

What's the matter with you? she scolded herself. *You know why he quit, Jill told you. If you wanted to help, why did you have to remind him of his own guilty conscience?*

She shivered, wishing she could take back the words that hung heavily between them. Doug unfurled his legs and stood up, reaching down to pull her to her feet. "You're cold. You need to go in, Amanda, it's too cold to sit out here."

She couldn't tell him that she wasn't shivering because she was cold. Their relationship was too new, and she didn't even know the direction that it was going. "What about you?" she finally squeezed through stiff lips. "Would you like to come in for some hot chocolate? Or I could make some sandwiches. We didn't get any dinner."

"No, I think it's better if we call it a night."

He stood over her, his hand lightly resting on her arm. "Maybe this wasn't such a good idea," he said softly, almost as if he were speaking to himself.

"What wasn't a good idea?" She raised her head, trying to bring his face into focus in the dim light.

He rubbed one hand over his eyes and emitted a low groan. His eyes narrowed, and Amanda froze, barely able to breathe in the face of such pain.

The groan changed to a throaty growl just before he grabbed her shoulders. His action startled her, but she didn't pull away, aware of the conflicting emotions coursing through his body. She felt safe with him, even as his lips pressed against hers with unrelenting force.

When he lifted his head, she met his gaze calmly. Her lips throbbed and she knew they were probably bruised, but she resisted the urge to touch them. Until he banished the shadows from his soul, he would have no room for her in his life.

His hands dropped to his sides, and he turned away from her. "I'm sorry, Amanda."

She touched his arm gently. "No apology necessary."

He swung around. "Thanks. I wish things were different."

Something in his tone alerted her. "Doug . . ."

He shook his head. "Amanda, you're a bright, beautiful young woman, and you deserve someone who doesn't have a lot of past baggage to bring with him. I thought things had changed, but tonight, at your parents' house and just now . . ." He jammed his hands into his pockets. "You don't need to go out with a man who isn't perfect, Amanda. You deserve better."

"Don't you think that should be my choice?"

His hand touched her cheek for a fleeting moment. "You don't know me, Amanda. I don't even know myself sometimes."

"Doug, nobody's perfect. I've got a lot of rough edges myself. Just ask my family," she offered, trying to inject a lighter mood into the dark conversation.

She felt his hesitation. A memory from their earlier meeting at the diner filtered through the fog in her brain and she jumped on it. "You did offer to help with the community building campaign. We could work together, get to know each other that way. Be friends."

She couldn't believe she was standing on her porch steps pleading with a man she had only met the day before. But she knew that she couldn't let him out of her life. Not yet. Not until she was sure that they had no future together.

After several long minutes, she saw him shake his head. "I know this is probably the coward's way out, but I don't think I would be much help on the campaign. I haven't been around for the past five years, so I wouldn't know who would help or who would be a hindrance."

His rejection hurt, but she wouldn't show it. "I understand."

"Thanks." He started down the sidewalk and then stopped. "I will take you up on your second offer."

She frowned, trying to remember what else she had said. "My second offer?"

He stepped back toward her. With his back to the light, she couldn't see his expression. She braced, wondering how else this man could turn her world upside down.

"To be friends," he said. "I could use a friend right now, Amanda."

She let her breath out slowly. "I'd like that."

"Okay." He placed his hands on her shoulders and turned her toward her front door. "Now, as one friend to another, it's time for you to go in. You're doing a great job pretending you're not cold, but even I'm starting to feel a chill."

She walked up the steps and dug her key out of her pocket. She could feel his presence behind her, waiting. Once the door was open, she turned around and waved at him. "Good night. I'll call you."

"Good night." He remained on the sidewalk until she clicked on the inside lights and shut the door.

She watched him walk the short distance to his car. The motor roared to life, and the car slid into the inky blackness of the night.

She locked the door and crossed the hallway to the bathroom. While the warm water filled the tub, she sat on the floor and leaned her head against the cool porcelain. *Now what?* she thought. *You've finally met the man who could very possibly be your soulmate, and he obviously found his mate years ago. I wonder if the gods planted a few ringers in the world just to keep things interesting.*

Bubbles floated around the room. She reached over and shut off the faucet. From outside the room, she could hear the phone ringing and knew her mother was checking on her. With a sigh, she stood up and answered the phone in her bedroom.

"You're there," her mother said.

"Yes, Mom." Amanda leaned against a chest of drawers. "It's not that far from your house."

"Are you all right? I know this evening didn't go as you planned. And he seemed such a nice young man."

Amanda bit back a grin. Her mother had no doubt already planned her wedding, only to see her dreams dashed when Doug left the house so soon after his arrival. "I'm fine, Mom. In fact, I've just run a bath, and I have a new book I want to start."

"Good idea. Get to bed early, and things will look brighter in the morning."

Amanda promised she would do that and hung up the phone. Gathering her nightgown and robe, she wondered if her mother truly believed that a good night's sleep was all it took to right the world. For as long as she could remember, Patricia Blake had advocated early nights for worried children.

She climbed into the tub and closed her eyes, letting the soothing water relax her strained muscles and drain away the tension from her shoulders. The book lay neglected on the floor.

When she saw the shriveled raisins that her toes had become, she climbed out, draining the cool water. She ran across the hall to her bedroom and dove under the thick comforter, pulling the blanket over her head and huddling in the warmth. Sleepy and warm, she curled into a ball and closed her eyes. Her fingers traced the pattern of her lips, reliving the kiss on the porch, and she hoped her mother's advice would prove sound.

Chapter Five

Amanda rode two blocks out of her way to avoid the car dealership the next morning. The office was blissfully dark when she unlocked it and she spent a quiet half hour before she heard anyone else arrive.

Megan popped her head into the open doorway. "Seems everything's in order again."

"Because I'm first in the office?" Amanda shook her head and waved her secretary/receptionist/friend out of the room. "You're starting to sound like Bob. Now, go, let me work in peace."

The main door creaked open again, and Megan glanced over her shoulder. She grinned at Amanda. "Sorry. The real thing's just arrived."

Amanda stifled her groan and bent her head over the stack of papers on her desk. Megan chuckled, and Amanda heard her walk down the hallway. "Good morning, Bob."

Bob's greeting didn't make it to Amanda's office, but she didn't have long to wait before he came down to give her one in person. "Morning, Amanda. Megan said you're busy, so I won't bother you."

"Thanks, Bob." Amanda scribbled another note on the long stack growing in front of her.

"Umm, Amanda."

She lifted her head. Bob stood in the doorway, a frown on his face. "What is it, Bob? Did you have trouble with the library commercial?"

"No, no, the actors worked out just great." He dropped his briefcase to the floor and advanced toward the desk, chewing on his lower lip. "Amanda, are you all right? I'm getting this awful reading . . ."

Amanda leaned her palms against her desk and pushed herself upright, suddenly tired of auras and worried friends and families. Bob's words stopped and his eyes widened.

She leaned forward, balancing her weight on her arms. "Listen, Bob, I appreciate your concern. But I don't think auras and all your other readings fit in the office. If you want to do readings for your friends during your time off, that's fine. But this is a place of business, and we have work to do."

His Adam's apple moved slowly up and down as he swallowed. "All right, Amanda. I'm sorry. It's just that . . ."

She lifted one hand, and his words trailed off. "Now, if you have the final report on the library account, I want to drop it off this morning."

"Of course, Amanda." He swung his briefcase onto a low table and snapped it open. "But I could take the report over and save you the trip." He pulled out a thick folder and rifled through the pages before selecting several of them. Handing them to Amanda, he added, "You don't need to be the messenger."

Amanda accepted the stack of papers and gave them a cursory glance. Bob did excellent work, and she knew his figures would be accurate. "No, it's fine. The director left a message yesterday that she wanted to go over another project."

"Okay." Bob slammed his briefcase closed. "And don't worry about the office. I'll keep working on the Forsythe case and take care of anything else that comes up."

This new businesslike attitude alarmed Amanda, and she wondered if she had created a new monster. "Just finish the Forsythe case, Bob. Megan will be here for anything else."

He leaned forward. "Yes, but she doesn't have the business acumen needed for executive decisions."

For the umpteenth time, she wondered why Bob hadn't gone into business for himself. With his flair for creative ideas and his knowledge of accounting and computers, he could have run his own successful company. She had asked him once, but he had only stated that he didn't like being in charge of other people.

You could fool me, she thought now, as she tried to extract a promise that he would let Megan handle the office. "She's here to make our job easier," Amanda said, "so that we can concentrate on the creative side of the business."

"That's true. Just remind her that I'm available if she needs any special expertise."

"We know that, Bob. We all know that." She rested her hand on his arm and slowly led him to the door. "Just concentrate on the Forsythe account."

After he left, she gathered up several large notebooks and a package of pens and stuffed them into her backpack. She was halfway down the hall when she remembered Bob's library report and she retraced her steps.

The phone rang as she stepped into her office. "I'm not available, Megan." She grabbed the folder and headed back down the hall.

"I'm sorry, Mrs. Blake, I don't know when she'll be back. Of course. Yes, I'll tell her." Megan jotted down some numbers while Amanda leaned over the desk. When she hung up, she handed the slip to Amanda.

"Thanks, Megan, you're a jewel." Amanda tucked the piece of paper into her pocket. "I should be back before lunch. Take any messages, and I'll try to return them this afternoon."

"Even that one?" Megan pointed toward Amanda's pocket. "Your mother sounded worried about you. Is something going on I should know about?"

"No." Amanda didn't say anything else, tugging her bike away from its spot against the wall. "You know how mothers can be."

"Yes, I do."

The meeting with Carolyn Banks, the library director, lasted an hour. She had finally received both permission and funds to launch a campaign highlighting the summer reading program. "The television station will run our spot during the local news," she explained to Amanda, "and the paper will run a notice several times before school's out."

Amanda jotted down dates and speakers for the program. Since the library had just received approval, she would have little time to develop a full-scale proposal. She flipped the pages of her daily planner, wondering how they could fit in one more campaign. "I can probably get something to you next week, but it won't be very complete."

"That's fine, Amanda. I know we've cut this close, but they didn't have any money before this last meeting." Carolyn leaned forward, her hands clasped on the desk. A book cart trundled by, one wheel squeaking. "The money came from an anonymous donor, so that we could encourage young people to read this summer."

Amanda smiled. "I see." They both had an idea of who the anonymous donor might be, a retired librarian who now sat on the library board. Her generous donations, culled from a small pension and a lifetime habit of living frugally, had appeared twice before to help with advertisement. The donations always arrived with only one string attached: "The spots have to provide positive encouragement for young people to read."

When the meeting was over, Amanda crossed the large main room and headed for the reference desk. She thought about the single stipulation she had received. The committee opposed to the community building had the same single-minded determination. While the anonymous donor allowed some flexibility in her thinking, as long as the main focus remained the same, the opposition seemed determined to uphold their own rigid ideal of family values without recognizing that other opinions could also be valid.

She shook her head and frowned. Somehow, she needed to show that the community building would support families without pulling them apart. Maybe some of the spots could combine grandparents and grandchildren together, letting the pictures speak for themselves. And one of them could show a family reunion being held at the center.

"Hi, Amanda, can I help you?"

Amanda shook her head, clearing her thoughts at the sound of the reference librarian's question. "Sorry, Mabel, I was thinking about one of my campaigns."

The older woman grinned. "Probably a good thing you do ride a bicycle, Amanda. With that wandering brain of yours, who knows what might happen if you drove a car?"

Amanda's thoughts shifted to Doug and his refusal to sell her a sports car. Was she destined to ride a bike forever?

"So, what can I do for you, Amanda?"

Amanda forced herself to focus on the business at hand. "I need to look at some old newspapers. From about five years ago."

"They'll be on microfiche." Mabel led the way to a wide cabinet and pulled open a drawer. "Do you know which months?"

"No. But the paper isn't that big. I should be able to spin through the pages pretty quickly."

Mabel loaded the microfiche reader, and Amanda dropped her backpack on the floor. "Thanks." She sat down and studied the first page.

"Let me know if you need anything else. That reel includes about four months worth of papers."

Amanda waited until Mabel walked away before spinning the knob. The obituaries were always near the end of the day's paper. She kept her eyes glued to the screen, watching for the distinctive heading.

The alphabetical listing at the beginning of each section sped up the task. She glanced at the names, searching for one that would be in the middle. The pages whizzed past.

Near the end of the first reel, a picture caught her eye. She slowed down and turned the wheel until she could see the subjects more clearly.

Doug. A younger Doug but Doug nonetheless. He wore a tuxedo and had his arms around a petite young woman whose eyes were full of adoration as she looked at him.

His own eyes shone with love as he smiled down at her. They were the center of the picture, with other couples dancing around them. The caption stated that "Dr. McCallister and his lovely wife, Mary, were part of the record-breaking crowd at the annual fundraising dance for the hospital."

Amanda stared at the couple. The black-and-white picture emphasized Doug's handsome coloring and showed him to advantage in his fancy clothes. Mary wore a light-colored gown, the dress clinging to her slight frame and swirling around her legs as she danced. Her hair curled around her face, accenting the delicate bone structure and the perfectly formed rosebud lips.

The expression on their faces captured Amanda's attention. Their love seemed to jump off the page, and she could see why the editor had chosen this picture. They were enjoying themselves, not only because they were at the dance, but because they were with each other. Other people were in the picture, but the viewer's eyes would be drawn to Dr. and Mrs. McCallister.

Amanda spun the dial and reached the end of the reel. The blank page stared at her, reminding her that she had never had anyone look at her with that much love in his eyes.

"And you probably never will," she grumbled. "You're not the small, fragile type." She pushed the rewind button and listened to the whirring of the machine as it spun the pages back to the beginning.

Just stop and go back to work, she told herself. She unhooked the reel and popped it into its box. She picked up the stack of boxes and then hesitated, half-raised in her seat.

She couldn't ask her sister any more information about Mary McCallister. If she wanted to know, she would have to discover the facts for herself.

The second reel slid onto the post easily. She flipped on the machine and turned the pages slowly. She stopped as a familiar name appeared in the middle of an article.

LOCAL DOCTOR SHARES SAFETY TIPS, the headline stated. The article detailed a visit local pediatrician, Dr. Doug McCallister, made to the elementary schools. He discussed, the article stated, safety concerns for home, school, and outside. His visit ended with him joining the students in a rousing version of "This Old Man," complete with safety tips that had the entire group doubled over with giggles.

Amanda grinned as she turned the lever. She could see the Doug she had met at the car dealership singing with a group of students. His sense of fun had been evident when he tried to dissuade her from buying a car.

Another headline slowed her down. This one stated that Dr. McCallister would be the featured speaker for a Parents as Teachers monthly meeting. He would answer questions about young children and their dietary needs. As she continued to scan the pages, she found references to his help with an elderly group that wanted to adopt "grandchildren," his participation in a community musical evening to raise funds for the hospital, and a workshop he co-sponsored for families on living healthy lives.

Intent on searching for his name, the words "Mary McCallister" leaped off the page at her. Her hand stilled, and she stared at the listing in the section of the paper reserved for area and local deaths.

Coppertown, MO—Mary Wheaton McCallister, 26, Coppertown, died at 1:55 p.m. Wednesday, July 16, as the result of a two-car accident. (A report can be found on page six.)

Amanda paused and stared at the picture accompanying the notice. Mary had been Amanda's age. She could imagine her, young, eager, excited about the coming baby.

She read through the rest of the short article. Mary had been born in Joplin, Missouri, and moved to Coppertown when she was seven, where she lived until she left for college. She had married Doug McCallister six years earlier, and he survived, in addition to her parents, a brother and a sister, all still living in the Joplin/Coppertown area. Contributions could be made to the pediatrics unit of the Coppertown Hospital.

Amanda turned the knob until she found the local accident reports. The small, local paper included a section from the police blotter and the lead article was headlined, LOCAL DOCTOR'S WIFE DIES IN CAR ACCIDENT.

The details were sparse, merely stating that a young man, who was uninjured, failed to stop at a stop sign. His car hit that of Mary McCallister, the wife of Dr. McCallister, a local pediatrician. She was declared dead at the scene, and obituary information appeared among the day's death reports.

Amanda clicked off the machine and rested her chin on her hands. She stared at the blank screen, seeing again the bright young face of Mary McCallister. Her smile had been sweet, almost shy, as if she didn't want the photographer to capture her image. Soft hair floated around her face, and Amanda knew the picture had been taken during a happy time of her life.

She rewound the film and carried the stack back to the reference desk. "Find what you need?" the librarian asked her.

Amanda nodded. "Thank you. See you later." She crossed the large room, giving an abstracted wave to the head librarian as she passed the main desk. Unlocking her bike, she pedaled back toward her office.

The articles proved Doug's commitment and involvement with the community. When he left, he had left more than just memories of his wife. His profession, his friends, his support had all been bound up in this small town. Leaving it would have been hard but coming back was probably even more difficult.

No doubt he had been pleased to find someone who didn't recognize him from his past life. Until her sister's disastrous announcement, he had been just another young man interested in a young woman. They should have learned each other's history gradually as they spent time together, bringing in relevant snippets until they knew what they needed to know. Instead, his past had come spilling out, rushing them into a more intense stage.

Amanda sighed and pushed her bike over the curb. Ronald held the door open for her and his face puckered in worry. "You okay, Miss Blake?"

She wiped a hand over her face, brushing away the deep thoughts that probably lined her face. "I'm fine. Just thinking about a new project we've been asked to do."

"You're doing a great job for the community." The security guard pushed the elevator button for her. "It's good to see a local company getting the money for advertising."

"I appreciate the vote of confidence." *I just wish everyone felt that way,* she added silently as the elevator doors closed.

Upstairs, Megan greeted her with a stack of phone messages. "Mrs. Carlson called and wants you to call back as soon as you get in." The secretary's voice was grim. "She didn't sound like she believed me when I said you weren't available."

"Mrs. Carlson?" Amanda swung her backpack from her shoulders and picked up the handful of messages, flipping through the slips.

"The leader of the opposition to the Willowton renovation."

Amanda glanced at Megan. "Mrs. Carlson? Who is she?"

"A very opinionated woman." Megan twirled a red curl around her finger. "I went to school with her daughters. They never went to any of the ball games or after school activities. Rory was my age, and she tried out for the marching band, thinking she could go to the ball games that way. Once her mom found out they traveled to the different games, she hired a private teacher for Rory and put an end to Rory's plans."

Amanda leaned one hip against the desk. "Where are the girls now?"

"They both escaped as soon as they could. Rory lives in Seattle and I think her sister, Candice, is on the west coast, too. Rory sends me a Christmas card every year," she explained, "and we keep up that way."

"Hmmm." Amanda pushed off from the desk and started down the hall. "If you have her address, why don't you bring it in? It might be helpful to have around."

She was almost to the doorway when Megan called her name. "I forgot. A Doug McCallister called just a few minutes ago. He wanted you to call as soon as you came in. He sounded urgent and mentioned that he wanted to talk to you about last night. Said he'd changed his mind about something."

Amanda's throat tightened. Doug had called while she was in the library reading about him. He'd had second thoughts and didn't even want to be friends.

She closed her office door and leaned against it, collecting her thoughts. After a moment, she straightened up and walked over to her desk. She would call Mrs. Carlson first and let the woman vent her feelings regarding the proposed project. Her personal life had never interfered with her business before, and she wouldn't let it now.

Squaring her shoulders and taking a deep breath, she dialed Mrs. Carlson's number.

Chapter Six

She drummed her fingers on the desk while she waited for the line to be answered. A horn sounded outside her window and she heard Bob ask Megan for a file. When the older man walked down the hallway, a scent of his after-shave floated into the room.

"Hello, Carlson residence," a weedy voice answered just as Amanda had decided to hang up.

Amanda scrambled to gather her thoughts back to the phone call. "Hello, is this Mrs. Carlson?"

"May I ask who's calling?"

"Amanda Blake, of Blake Visions. I'm returning her call from this morning."

When the voice replied that she would get Mrs. Carlson, Amanda glanced at the note Megan had written at the bottom of the memo. Mrs. Carlson wanted to discuss her concerns with Ms. Blake and make a counter-proposition.

Amanda frowned. A counter-proposition? What did that mean? She was hired by the city to advertise the coming building and help with fundraising proposals. She didn't have any say in whether the building became a park or community building. Her only responsibility was to provide the city with advertising spots and encourage donations from the community for the renovation.

"Miss Blake?"

The voice that drifted over the phone sounded strong and confident. Amanda could imagine her forcing her daughters to stay home. Just the two syllables emanated force and the expectation that she would be obeyed.

Amanda sat up straighter. Her clients usually came into the office with specific ideas for their campaigns until her expertise and quiet confidence convinced them that their suggestions needed to be modified. She was used to working with difficult clients. This woman sounded no different.

"Yes, this is Amanda Blake. I understand you wanted to talk with me about the Willowton renovation."

"There should be no renovation," the woman stated firmly. "The building should be razed and a park developed on the land."

"I understand your position, Mrs. Carlson, but the city feels a community building would suit the needs of the people better."

"Hummph." Mrs. Carlson paused, and Amanda waited, knowing that she had only touched the tip of the iceberg.

She didn't have long to wait. "Miss Blake, I realize that your job is to present the plans as they are developed, help organize fundraisers for the project, and share positive news about the building. I will offer you double what the city is paying if you will withdraw from the city's project and come to our side."

Amanda blinked. Double the city's proposal? The figures were available at the city offices, so she didn't doubt Mrs. Carlson was aware of the amount of money involved. Mrs. Carlson must feel very strongly about the project if she was willing to part with that kind of money.

"I appreciate the offer, Mrs. Carlson," Amanda said softly, "but I didn't take on the project for the money."

"I see." Mrs. Carlson's voice had a hard edge to it. "And no amount will tempt you to change your position?"

"I'm afraid not. The community building would be an asset to the city, and we already have a number of parks."

Silence stretched over the line before Mrs. Carlson cut into Amanda's thoughts. "I hope you don't regret your decision, Miss Blake. If you should change your mind, please let me know within the next week."

Before Amanda had a chance to assure her that she wouldn't change her mind, the woman hung up the phone. Amanda stared at the receiver for several seconds and then dropped it into the cradle.

Megan burst into the room. "So, what happened? Did she threaten you?"

Amanda tipped her head back at Megan's eager questions. "Where did you come from? Were you eavesdropping?"

"Of course not." Megan perched on the edge of the low table. "But I could tell when you hung up the phone. The light went off on my phone," she explained.

"Oh, good. So now you're timing my calls?"

Megan grinned at Amanda's teasing. "Come on, Amanda. Tell me. Should Ronald walk me out to my car tonight?"

Amanda sobered. Mrs. Carlson had been cold, and her voice oozed power. She chewed on her lower lip. "I don't think we should joke about this, Megan. For some reason, she's very upset about this renovation." She hesitated, wondering how much she should divulge to her secretary.

"Did she threaten you?" Megan's eyes widened, and she leaned forward.

Amanda shook her head. "Not really. But she did offer to double the city's figures if I would resign and go to work for them."

Megan leaned back and whistled. "Double? Wow, Amanda, we could stop worrying about bills for a while."

The constant scrambling to pay the bills was a concern, but Amanda wouldn't sacrifice her principles to ensure that the electricity or phone bill was paid. "No, Megan, I didn't start this company to get rich. I wanted to give something back to the community, and the renovation is more important than another park."

Megan pushed herself up and grinned. "I'll remind you of your high principles the next time you're complaining about the lack of funds in the bank."

"Megan . . ." Amanda warned, but Megan just waved a hand over her shoulder and walked out the door.

Amanda leaned her elbows on the desk and stared at the stack of messages that still needed answering. Doug's phone number seemed to jump from the page, and she finally picked up the phone and quickly punched out the numbers.

"Foster's," a young voice answered.

Amanda cleared her throat. "Doug McCallister, please."

"One moment."

Music played over the receiver while she waited, her thoughts alternating between a desire to see him again and a wish to have her normal life back. When Doug's voice broke through the cheerful strains of a popular tune, identifying himself, she fought down the urge to slam down the phone and not hear him pull out of her life forever.

"Doug McCallister," he repeated.

She swallowed. "Sorry, I was looking over some letters while I waited," she invented quickly, hoping he couldn't hear the thudding of her heart over the phone cable.

"No problem. I was in the back lot, and it took me a few minutes to get to the phone." His voice lowered. "I think I just sold your sports car."

"It's not my sports car," she retorted. "Remember, I'm the one who needs a minivan."

His laugh didn't sound like a man ready to drop her from his life. She relaxed in her chair. "Megan said you called this morning."

"Yes. I've been thinking about our conversation last night."

"Oh?" Amanda sat up.

"I *will* help you on your campaign. I didn't move back here to hide from my past, and working with your company might be a good way to ease back into the community."

Amanda let out a small sigh of relief. "I'd like that, Doug. We can use all the help we can get." She was tempted to tell him about Mrs. Carlson's offer but decided to wait until she knew him better.

"I also owe you a dinner. You missed out on something that smelled wonderful last night."

"Mom is a great cook," Amanda admitted. *And so are Jill and Christine,* she added silently. *Surely I could do this if I just applied myself.*

"So? Are you free for dinner tonight? I thought I'd make reservations at Traletti's."

Amanda tapped her fingers on the desk. If they went out for dinner, they could easily be swamped with friends of hers curious about the man she was with, or former friends of Doug's, eager to know what he was doing back in town.

She made a quick decision. "Why not come over to my house for dinner? That way we could talk about the campaign without a lot of interruptions."

"Are you sure? I mean, this is supposed to be my invitation."

"But you missed a homecooked meal by my mother. The least I can do is cook one for you."

"All right, if you're sure."

She wasn't, she didn't have a clue about the dinner menu, but she couldn't risk having dinner with him in a public place. She didn't know everyone in Coppertown, but Traletti's was a popular spot for her friends. A quiet meal at her house would give them the perfect opportunity to get to know each other.

They decided on 7:30. When he rang off, she broke the connection and then quickly dialed her sister's number.

"Jill, I know this sounds crazy, but I need something fabulous to fix for dinner that even I can't mess up."

"Amanda, is that you?"

Amanda groaned and pulled out a tablet. "Yes, Jill. Listen, I'm cooking dinner tonight for a friend, and I need something I can pull together between now and 7:30."

"That's doesn't leave much time, Amanda. Why don't you just go out for dinner?"

"Jill, please, this is important to me."

She could almost hear her sister's thoughts whirring around in her lovely head. "Dr. McCallister?"

Amanda wondered why she hadn't remembered her sister's uncanny ability to discern her plans. While Jill had always been the one to save Amanda from her mother's interference, she also required her pound of flesh.

"Jill, listen, you're right, this is a dumb idea. It's already 3:00; I'd have to go shopping, pick up the house, I don't have any nice dishes. Sorry I bothered you." She could find something at the store that she could whip up in a few hours. She didn't need her big sister's help.

"Amanda, come on, I'll help you. Just let me think a minute."

Amanda doodled on the tablet. On the other end of the line, she could hear Jill flipping pages. Her sister collected cookbooks like some people collected rocks. "Okay," Jill said, "it needs to be something that looks great but doesn't take a lot of time. Mmmm."

Amanda waited. Once her sister started on a project, there was no hope of interrupting her. They had all inherited the trait from their one-track mother.

"I've got it. Paella. It's easy to make, and you can add anything you want to it."

"Py—what?"

"Py-a-yuh," Jill said patiently. "Mom makes it all the time. Rice, seafood, artichoke hearts."

Amanda vaguely remembered a dish her mother had served during colder weather when the family gathered at the house. Her brother had picked out the artichoke hearts before Patricia ordered him to save some for the rest of the family.

"Okay, what do I need to buy?" She held her pencil poised over the table.

"Tell you what. I'll meet you at the store and we can shop together."

"Jill—"

"Amanda, you can't prepare a gourmet dinner in less than four hours by yourself. Besides, if you're going to cook for Dr. McCallister, you need all the help you can get. Mary was a wonderful cook."

Maybe it wasn't too late to call Traletti's. Surely they wouldn't be that busy on a week night. "A simple tossed salad would probably work," her sister murmured, continuing to add to the menu and oblivious to Amanda's conflicting emotions. "Green leaf lettuce looks pretty, and you can add cherry tomatoes, carrots—"

"I know how to make a salad," Amanda interrupted. She glanced at her watch. "Are you sure I can make all of this before tonight?"

"Of course you can. I'll meet you at the store in thirty minutes."

The pile of phone messages and letters to sign beckoned her from the corner of the desk. "I'm not sure I can get away that soon."

"Amanda, what's the use of being your own boss if you can't sneak away early every now and then? Be there in thirty minutes. I'll start picking up items in the produce section."

Resigned to the younger sister role she always assumed when confronted by her older siblings, Amanda agreed. She didn't have a choice. Jill would come to the office and get her if she didn't arrive at the store.

After they hung up, Amanda sifted through the rest of the phone messages. Most concerned routine questions that she could deal with in the morning. She gathered up the stack of papers, stuffed them into an empty folder, and crammed it into the top drawer of her desk.

As she neared the front office, she cringed. Not only did she come into the office first, she also left last. Megan and Bob would want to know what was going on.

And what will I tell them? she thought. *I could say I'm going out to work on the Willowton campaign, but then they'd want to know more details.*

She slung her backpack over her shoulders and lifted her head. She owned the company. They worked for her. If she wanted to leave early or take a two-hour lunch, that was her business. Their projects wouldn't suffer, and so she would tell them if anyone asked.

Ready with her answers, she was surprised when Megan only wished her a good evening. "Bob's finishing the Forsythe account and said he should have the final report to you tomorrow morning." She turned back to the letter she was typing.

Astonished at this lack of concern on her secretary's part, Amanda opened and closed her mouth several times. Megan lifted her head. "Is there something else?"

"No," Amanda finally managed to say, wondering if she was the crazy one. Why had she thought an early departure would make such a difference to her staff?

"I'll leave any messages that come on your desk. Good night."

Amanda pushed her bike down the hallway. While she waited for the elevator, the lawyer from next door came out of his office. "Hi, Amanda. Early evening?"

"Yes," she said, waiting for his comment.

"You deserve it. Have a good time." He headed down the hall to the conference room.

Ronald waved goodbye, and she strapped on her helmet. Maybe she *was* working too hard. No one seemed to mind that she was taking on early night and, except for her desire to stem unnecessary questions, she would probably go home early more often.

"Otherwise, why own your own business?" she muttered as she cut across the parking lot.

Her sister had just parked her minivan when Amanda arrived. She locked her bike in the rack near the front door and waited for Jill. Her six-year-old niece followed her sister.

"Sorry, Amanda. Luke went over to a friend's house after school and Anna's friend wasn't home yet."

Amanda bent down and hugged her niece. "It's okay. You can help us shop, can't you, Anna?"

"Mom says you're cooking for a man who's coming over."

Amanda scowled at her sister. Jill lifted her hands in a delicate shrug. "She overheard part of my conversation with Mom and I had to explain what was going on."

"You told Mom?" Amanda demanded.

Soft color rushed into Jill's cheeks. "She called just as I was going out the door. I didn't mean to tell her, Amanda, and I didn't tell her who."

Amanda groaned. "It doesn't matter. Ten to one, she'll call as soon as we get home."

With Jill's expert help, the shopping didn't take long. Anna selected tomatoes for the salad and added cucumbers, carrots, sprouts, mushrooms, and red onions to the growing pile of groceries. At the meat counter, Jill agonized over the right size of shrimp until Amanda pointedly looked at her watch.

"Okay, okay." Jill finally added the last ingredient and turned the cart toward the checkout lines.

"When we get home, you can wash the vegetables for the salad," she told Anna as the stockboy loaded bags into the back of her van. "I'll make the custard and Amanda, you can start organizing the paella ingredients."

The phone rang as they carried in the last bag. Amanda made a face at her sister when she heard Patricia's voice. Jill grinned and plucked the bag out of Amanda's arms.

"Hello, Mother," Amanda said. She leaned on the counter and kicked off her shoes.

Jill scooped them up and carried them into the bedroom. "We have enough to do without new messes," she muttered.

Amanda stuck out her tongue and barely heard her mother's question. "No, Mom, I don't need any more help. I'm just making dinner."

"Jill said she gave you the recipe for paella. Do you think that's a good idea?" her mother asked.

"You just throw a bunch of ingredients together and let it simmer," Amanda said. "How hard can that be?"

From behind her, she heard Jill groan. She swung around and batted her eyelashes at her sister. Jill laughed and tossed a sponge at her. Amanda neatly caught it, juggling it from hand to hand while she listened to her mother.

Jill reached over and pulled the phone out of her hand. "Listen, Mom, Amanda can't talk right now. She needs to finish picking up the house and get the dinner going." She listened for a minute and nodded. "I'll tell her."

She hung up the phone and wiped her hands on the beach towel she had wrapped around her waist in place of an apron. "Tell me what?" Amanda asked suspiciously.

"Mom wants you to call and give her all the details tomorrow," Jill said innocently.

"Jill!"

Jill tipped her head toward her young daughter, who stood on a stool carefully washing tomatoes and carrots. With a frustrated snap of a dish towel, Amanda grabbed a knife and whacked away at the chicken Jill had placed on the cutting board.

Jill laid her hand over Amanda's wrist. "Neatly, Amanda. You don't want it to look like a savage cooked this meal."

"I feel pretty savage right now," Amanda muttered under her breath, her eyes going to her niece. "There's no reason for me to call Mom tomorrow. I'm just having dinner with a potential business associate."

"A business associate?" Jill paused in her mixing. "We're going to all this work for a business associate?"

"Well, it was your idea. I just wanted something that was easy and didn't look like it came from the frozen food section."

Amanda carefully cut the chicken into bite-sized pieces, being careful not to catch her sister's eye. When Jill didn't move, Amanda peeked at her from under her lashes.

"I thought since you brought him to Tim's party the other night, you were dating him," Jill hissed under her breath.

"He's helping with the Willowton project," Amanda said. A smug feeling of satisfaction settled in her stomach. Her sister actually believed she felt nothing for Doug.

"Mommy, something smells funny."

Jill moaned and grabbed the pan of caramel from the stove. She dipped in her finger and tasted the mixture. "You're sure he's just a business associate?"

Amanda nodded. "Then this should be fine." Jill moved the pan to a cool burner.

"Jill! I still want this dinner to go well."

"It's not burnt or anything." Her sister drizzled the caramel into custard cups. "I just thought that you and Doug—"

"Who's Doug?"

They both turned at Anna's piping voice. She had hopped down from her stool and now stood shoulder to hip with Amanda.

Jill leaned down and kissed her daughter's cheek. "A friend of Aunt Amanda's." She cracked eggs in a businesslike manner, her expression bland as she looked at Amanda. "A business friend."

"Then why are we fixing this fancy dinner? Aunt Amanda doesn't cook like this."

Amanda grinned at her forthright comment and scooped up her niece, giving her a big hug. "Maybe not usually, Anna, but don't you think I could if I wanted to?"

Anna leaned back and studied Amanda, her eyes narrowed in concentration. "I guess so. Daddy said you're pretty smart and if you can follow directions, you can cook."

"Thank you for the vote of confidence, sweetheart."

She set Anna back on her feet and picked up her knife. "She's right, though, Jill. I should be cooking this on my own. Otherwise, I'm showing myself under false pretenses."

Jill measured the egg mixture into the custard cups. "Maybe. But if you went to a restaurant, somebody else would cook the meal. Just pretend that we're the hired help."

Amanda laughed. "Somehow I have a feeling I'm not going to like the bill that you're going to send me."

Chapter Seven

By the time the custards came out of the oven, the table had been set with the good china Jill had brought with her. Amanda refused the crystal candlesticks, and under the circumstances, Jill finally agreed they would be too much. Anna's zealously tossed salad sat on the bottom shelf of the refrigerator, and the creamy custards rested on the top shelf.

"At 6:30, start the paella," Jill directed, looking over the list she had posted on the refrigerator. "You've already browned the chicken, so you can just add the other ingredients and let it simmer. When he gets here, you just have to bring out the salad and drinks, and the paella will be ready when you are."

"I know, I know." Amanda pushed her sister toward the door. "You've told me at least half a dozen times, and I have the list on the fridge." She rested her hands on her sister's shoulders and smiled at her. "Thank you very much. When I called you, I wasn't expecting this much help."

Jill kissed her cheek. "Take a shower and rest for a few minutes. The house looks great, and dinner will be wonderful." She leaned forward and whispered, "He's really nice. You could mix business with pleasure."

"Are you telling Aunt Amanda secrets?" Anna demanded. She tugged on her mother's sleeve.

"No, I'm not." She clasped her daughter's hand in her own and headed for the door. "And don't worry about Mom. If you want, we can have dinner at my house tomorrow, and then you can answer her questions with the rest of us in support."

"Oh, now that's a pleasant thought. A complete Blake inquisition."

Jill grinned. "I'd mark your bill paid in full."

Amanda yanked the door open and pointed a finger outside. "Go. You're going to drive me crazy."

After the door closed behind them, Amanda raced into the bedroom. She dug through her clothes, wondering if she should try the blue dress tonight. Her mother wouldn't see her and the dress *did* look good on her. . . .

Showered and wearing the blue dress, she headed for the kitchen and her sister's instructions. She wrapped a huge bath towel around her waist, wishing she had an apron. She made a mental note to ask Jill where she could buy one. Her sister wore one every time she cooked. The thought of paella on her skirt kept her movements slow and steady.

Her mind wandered to her conversation with Mrs. Carlson after she covered the skillet and set the timer for twenty minutes. Megan's comments about the daughters returned, and she wondered if she should contact them. She never had liked the dirty campaigning that often appeared during election times and encouraged her clients to stick with the issues and their own strengths. "Often, making negative remarks about the opponent leaves that name in their mind instead of your own," she would tell her clients.

Now all she could think about was Mrs. Carlson and her opposition. For some reason, the older woman hated the thought of providing a spot for young people to gather, and yet her own daughters had taken the first opportunity to run away from her. Could that information be used to help the renovation project? And how could she use it and still follow her own principles?

"She's like a fire-breathing dragon," Amanda said. She plumped a pillow on the couch and sat down on the edge of the cushion.

"A dragon. She's sure dragging me down."

The image of a fire-breathing dragon carrying a load of people caught her imagination. "Dragging me down," Amanda repeated. She reached for a pad of paper she kept near the couch and sketched a rough drawing of a dragon.

"Is summer dragging you down?" she murmured, her mind shifting to the library program. "Hop onboard and join the summer reading program."

She sketched and erased, adding books to her earlier scenes. The dragon's tiny wings carried him over a small town, complete with swimming pool, playground and burning sun. At the edge of the picture, she added a library with tall, shining towers.

Satisfied with her start on the library project, she dropped the paper on the coffee table and stretched. She rubbed the back of her shoulders, wiggling the stiff muscles.

The doorbell rang and she blinked, trying to bring her thoughts back to the present. At the second ring, she jumped to her feet and opened the door.

Doug stood on the front porch, a bouquet of spring flowers in his hand. "Hi." His brows drew together. "You were expecting me, weren't you? It's 7:30."

Her eyes widened and she clapped her hand to her mouth. "Oh, no." She raced across the living room and into the kitchen.

Jerking the lid off the electric skillet, she stared at the dried rice and chicken. "Oh, no!" She pressed her hand to her forehead and stared at the ruins of the dinner she had planned.

"Is that dinner?"

"Was," she muttered.

She jerked the plug out of the wall and carried the skillet across the room. She dumped the carefully prepared ingredients into the trash can, wrinkling her nose at the scorched smell of the chicken. *At least I didn't add the artichoke hearts,* she thought sadly.

"What was the matter with it?"

She held up the burned-on remnants of rice. "I forgot what I was doing. It shouldn't have cooked as long as it did without the other ingredients." She knew she sounded forlorn but she had wanted to make a good impression. *Instead, he's lucky he didn't find the house burned down around my ears,* she thought.

He took the pan out of her hand and placed it in the sink before wrapping his long fingers around her now empty hand. "It's all right, Amanda. I appreciate the effort. We can go get a bite to eat."

Her hand quivered. He filled the tiny space of her kitchen, his head only inches from the light hanging in the middle of the room, his dark eyes crinkling at the corners even as he expressed his regret. His aftershave, a softer, more masculine version of the sports scent that Bob wore, invaded her senses, driving out the burning smell of the rice and chicken and replacing it with a hunger that food wouldn't satisfy.

"I do have a salad and custard that didn't get damaged," she said quickly, stepping away from his dangerous touch.

He cocked one eyebrow at her. "And bread," she added to the meager menu, hoping the loaf in the bread box was still fresh.

"That sounds good."

She grinned at his polite response. "Okay, you're right. It's not much to offer for dinner." She opened the cupboard above the sink and poked around its contents. "I could make spaghetti. Jill left a package of her meatballs in the freezer, and if I cook it in the microwave, it shouldn't take too much time."

"Sounds better." He unbuttoned his jacket and draped it over a chair before unbuttoning his cuffs and rolling up his sleeves. "Show me a pan and I'll cook up a mean batch of noodles."

She pointed to a cupboard next to the stove and handed him the package of spaghetti noodles. While they cooked, he told her about the young man who bought the sports car that afternoon.

"He's just finishing his freshman year in college, and he needs a car for his summer job."

"He's buying a car *before* he gets a summer job?" Amanda stirred the meatballs into the sauce and glanced over her shoulder at him.

"He has a little money set aside." Doug scooted around her with the pan of water and placed it on the stove.

"For a sports car." Amanda popped the saucepan into the microwave and closed the microwave door. She leaned her hips against the sink. "I never had money to set aside for a car."

"Is that why you ride a bike?" Doug rested one hip against the sink, only inches away from her.

Heat from the stove and Doug's close range crept up her arms. She resisted the urge to pull her hand away from the sink, away from the strong hand with the dark hairs that marched up his arm and disappeared under the pristine white of his rolled-up shirtsleeve. "That and the fact that I like to feel the wind on my face when I'm riding," she said, trying to regain the topic of conversation and a measure of control over her senses. "I'm not hemmed in by some metal cage when I'm traveling around town."

Doug lifted his hands in surrender. "Okay, okay, I give up. I'll quit my job tomorrow."

Amanda laughed and grabbed his wrists, pulling his hands down to waist level. "You asked why *I* don't have a car. That doesn't mean a lot of other people wouldn't love to buy one of your contraptions."

His hands shifted in her grasp until his fingers were laced with hers. His smile slowly melted away, and she found her breath catching in her throat at the serious expression in his eyes.

Time stopped. She noticed the way his lashes curled around his eyes and perfectly matched the color of his eyebrows. The steam from the spaghetti pan had loosened the hair around his face and several strands curled boyishly around his forehead.

His thumbs lightly rubbed her wrists and kindled a warmth in her that owed nothing to the boiling water on the burner. When the microwave timer dinged, she dragged her eyes reluctantly from his face and stepped away from his touch.

"I can't burn two dinners in one night." She hoped her words sounded casual enough and hid the sudden erratic beating of her heart.

"We would definitely have to go out then." Doug reached around her and unhooked the potholders from their place on the wall. "The whole house could burn down this time."

She hid her hurt feelings under a chuckle as she carried the dish of spaghetti sauce to the table. Jill wouldn't have burned the dinner. Mary wouldn't have, either. From everything she had discovered, Mary had been the perfect doctor's wife, willing to help him with community affairs, charming to the many people they had to meet, a wife perfectly able to have dinner waiting for him when he came home from the hospital.

"Voila!" He plopped the bowl of noodles in the middle of the table with a flourish. Amanda added the salad and bread and poured water into their glasses, using an etched glass pitcher Jill had loaned her for the occasion.

"Madam, your dinner awaits." He held out her chair, and her earlier cheerful mood returned. They were business associates bordering on friends, nothing more, and friends made the best of the times they could be together. She would follow his lead and ignore the episode in the kitchen.

The salad tasted delicious, and Amanda made a mental note to compliment her niece on her culinary abilities. *Maybe she can give me lessons,* she thought with an inward chuckle. Doug passed her the bread, and she buttered a slice. "Where did you go to medical school?"

The question popped out before she considered the implications. He handed her the noodles, and she wondered if he would answer her. "University of Missouri in Columbia," he finally said.

"I did, too!" Had they crossed paths without knowing it?

He dashed the possibility away. "I was probably finished before you started."

"True. I graduated two years ago." *I started a year before Mary died, she realized, during their last happy year together.*

He asked her about her college memories, and if her courses helped in the real world of business. Whenever she asked about his own remembrances, he deftly shifted the topic back to her without answering any of her queries.

After they finished dinner, he stacked the dishes and carried them into the kitchen. "You don't have to do that," she protested.

"I don't mind. The least I can do is help with the dishes after that delicious meal you cooked."

Her remorse at the unexpected turn of events intensified. "I didn't make anything except the spaghetti sauce," she confessed. "And you saw me take that out of a jar."

"The salad?"

"My six-year-old niece."

"The custard?"

"My sister Jill."

He hesitated. "But you were making the paella?"

"Oh, yes, and you saw how successful that was."

He tapped his index finger against his lips and she waited anxiously for him to say something. "Well, we can't all be cooks," he said, turning on the faucet and adding dish soap to the warm water.

"I was working on an idea for a new project," she explained as she pulled out a dishrag and towel. "I forgot about the time."

"Sounds like a reasonable explanation. Will it need much work?"

"It's still in the rough stages, but I think I have a workable plan for the library summer reading program."

While he washed and she dried the dishes, she shared her ideas about the dragon. She didn't mention Mrs. Carlson, her inspiration for the idea. The woman was causing her problems with the Willowton House project, but she refused to stoop to her level. She wouldn't talk about her behind her back.

When the last dish was put away, Doug took the dish towel from her hand, snapped it, and laid it over the counter to dry. He tucked her arm under his and led her to the living room.

"A wonderful dinner, Amanda, no matter how it came to be."

He sat down on the couch, and she sat in the easy chair across from him. She needed distance. Just the lighting of her hand on his arm accelerated the pace of her heart.

"Thanks to you. If you hadn't come around when you did, who knows what might have happened in that kitchen."

He chuckled. "That's what friends are for, right? To help you out of tight spots."

She nodded. His words reiterated what she had forced herself to think about earlier. She would just have to push down these strange sensations that kept cropping up whenever she was around him. They would do nothing but embarrass him if she ever acknowledged them, and she didn't want to lose his friendship.

He stretched out his legs and laced his hands behind his head. "Now, tell me about your campaign. How can I help you?"

She listed the different organizations that were already supporting them. "We've contacted the hospitals and doctors in the area, hoping that they will add their voice. Until the park group came along, we didn't even have to vote on the issue, but now they've received enough names on their petitions to call for a referendum."

"That's next Tuesday, isn't it?"

She nodded. "And the fundraiser dance is planned for the following Friday. We made all the arrangements at least six weeks ago, before this group even made its plans known."

"Rather quick for the ballot, isn't it?"

"Seems they've been working on it for quite a while in secret," she said drily. "As soon as the first article about the gift to the city appeared in the paper, petitions about the use of the land were circulated."

"Do you have any idea who's behind all of this, or why?"

She tucked her feet under her and leaned her head against the back of the chair. "We know who, but I can't figure out why."

"Who?"

The names weren't secret. He could find out by reading the names listed at the bottom of any of the newspaper ads they were running. "A Mrs. Ruth Carlson. Her husband is an international lawyer and out of town, and even the country, most of the time. All I know about her is that she's an older woman with enough money to fight this issue." And she makes veiled threats over the telephone.

"I'll ask around, see if anyone knows why she's against the community building. My cousin knows a lot about the people around here, and we hear things at the dealership." He grinned. "I'll be discreet, not let anyone know that I'm working for the other side's advertising agency."

"Thank you. I know there's a lot of curiosity about her motives. At the school board meeting the other night, someone asked what we were doing to stop their plans. When I mentioned that we were only hired to do the fundraising projects and promote the proposal, they wanted to know why we couldn't make sure the park idea was tossed out."

He rubbed his hand over his chin. "In a convoluted way, it does make sense." She gave him a questioning look. "You're hired to promote the project, and getting rid of the opposition would obviously promote it."

" 'Getting rid of the opposition,' " she repeated. "That sounds very democratic. How do you suppose Blake Visions could do that?" She plopped her hands on her hips, her eyes narrowed. "We're a public relations firm, not hired guns."

He laughed and leaned forward, his hands on his knees. "Now wait a minute, Amanda. We're supposed to be on the same side. I'm just explaining why I think some of the community members would expect you to . . ." He stopped and frowned, then raised both hands, palms up. "I don't know how else to say it. Get rid of the opposition!"

She took pity on him. "Well, it would make my job easier. If I could find a way to stop them, I'd do it. I think the vote will be in favor of the building idea, but you never know. People may think that the opposition is too small to worry about and not vote. The next thing you know, we have another park and no building."

"What do you want me to do? Besides listening for gossip."

"Doug!" Exasperation forced his name out. "That's not the way we do business."

"I know. But you can learn a lot by listening." He leaned closer and lowered his voice to a conspiratorial tone. "For instance, did you know the school board wants to eliminate the junior high and use a middle school approach instead?"

"Yes. And if you read the paper, you'd know that they've been working on this plan for the past two years."

She laughed at the injured look on his face and patted his hand. "It's okay, Doug. You haven't been back very long. Once you get into small-town living again, you'll be able to tell when you should listen to gossip and when it's just that, gossip."

He glanced at his watch and jumped to his feet. "I didn't realize how late it was. I need to get going, and you need your sleep, too."

She scrambled out of her chair, startled by his abrupt mood swing. "It's all right. I've stayed up late before."

He grabbed his jacket from the chair in the kitchen. "I do need to go, Amanda. I had a wonderful time." He paused at the door, his hand on the knob. "You didn't tell me exactly how I can help. What if I stop by your office tomorrow so we can go over some particulars?"

She could imagine the looks that Megan and Bob would exchange if Doug showed up in the office. Even though she didn't believe in Bob's ability to read auras, her secretary would quickly note that Amanda's interest in the handsome doctor-turned-car dealer revolved around more than a campaign to build a community building.

"I'll call you," she said.

He frowned. "Is that a brush-off?" he asked, his voice losing all of its earlier teasing tone.

"No!" She didn't understand why he was so upset. What did she say? "I *will* call you. It's just that . . ." she tried to think of a realistic reason that wouldn't reveal the truth.

"Never mind. Just let me know what you want me to do." He opened the door and paused, running a gentle finger down the side of her jaw. "I did have a wonderful time, Amanda."

Her skin tingled at his soft touch and his husky words. When the door closed behind him, she leaned against it, listening to his fading footsteps before she clicked off the lights. She headed toward her bedroom with one hand pressed against her chin and the phantom touch of his hand.

Chapter Eight

Sleep restored her equilibrium. As she rode her bike to the office, she reminded herself that she didn't need a man around to be successful, that adding Doug to her list of friends was more than adequate. Her energies and efforts had built Blake Visions, without the support of anyone else. Her parents and siblings might feel it necessary to have someone by their sides, but she could succeed very well on her own.

Dinner at her sister's proved to be a tactical event. Jill and Christine kept the conversation centered around Tim's upcoming wedding, begging Jenette for every detail the shy young woman could provide them. Patricia tried several times to break into the conversation and steer it toward Amanda's evening, but her older daughters manipulated her with their own skills.

Amanda complimented both her sister and niece for their share of the meal. When asked about the main course,

Amanda shrugged with what her sisters took to be quiet modesty and replied, "As well as could be expected," refusing to be drawn out anymore. When she kissed her mother goodnight, she could see the questions still swarming in her mind, but Patricia only patted her cheek and wished her a pleasant night's sleep.

For the next three days, she remembered her mother's wish at the odd hours she did drop off to sleep. She had little time to do much more than think about Doug, and then for only a few moments. Bob went home the day after her ill-fated dinner with a serious head cold that turned into the flu. With Bob away from the office and Sierra and Mark active with the community building project, she and Megan worked overtime to keep up with the other accounts.

Near the end of the third day, Megan plopped onto the couch in Amanda's office. "I can't do much more of this."

Amanda finished stuffing a letter into its envelope and sealed it. "We shouldn't have to. I talked to Bob this afternoon, and he's certain he can come back tomorrow."

"Thank goodness." Megan flung one arm over the back of the couch and dangled her legs over the arm rest. "I'm going to soak in the hottest tub I can stand. My body's aching."

"Go ahead and go home. I can take care of the rest of things."

Megan tipped her head back. "Are you sure? I could probably stand another few minutes."

"No, go." Amanda reached over and pulled Megan to her feet. "Go before I have to carry you home. And you know I just have my bike."

Megan headed for the door and then paused, leaning against the doorjamb. "Oh, I forgot. A message came this afternoon while you were at the bank."

"Oh?" Amanda lifted her head from the stack of notes she was sorting for the next day.

"That Doug guy, McCallister?" Megan wrinkled her nose. "I know that name, but I can't remember why."

Amanda was thankful she was sitting down. She had convinced herself that she didn't need anyone else, but the sound of his name was having an incredible effect on her body. "Did he say anything in particular?" she asked casually.

"No, just mentioned that he hadn't heard from you and wondered if you'd given any more thought to how he could help."

Amanda released her breath slowly. He was just someone helping with a campaign. They received calls like that all of the time.

"McCallister." Megan shook her head. "I know that name. It'll drive me crazy until I can figure it out."

Amanda hesitated for just a moment. "He used to live here," she offered softly, unable to trust her voice to add any more.

Megan grinned. "That's it then. One of my brothers probably knew him. I'll have to ask them, or I won't be able to sleep with that name floating around in my head."

Join the club, Amanda thought. "He's going to help with the community building project," she managed.

"Great. We can use all the help we can get. At least Mrs. Carlson hasn't phoned recently." Megan waved cheerfully and Amanda soon heard her heels tapping down the hall-way.

She rocked gently in her chair. Doug had called. He had said he wouldn't, but then, she had promised she would get back to him. He hadn't seemed like an impatient man. Of course, what did she really know about him?

Her right hand strayed toward the telephone. Her left hand drummed a pencil on the desk. What to do? What to do?

"You didn't become your own boss by being wishy-washy," she muttered. She grabbed the receiver and quickly dialed the number for the car dealership.

"Foster's."

"Is Doug McCallister there, please?"

"I'm sorry, Mr. McCallister left for the evening. May I take a message? Or someone else would be happy to help you."

Amanda swallowed. "No, thank you." She hung up the phone quickly, pressing her hand against her throat before she grabbed the stack of papers and forced herself to read through them.

Ronald's evening replacement held the door open for her when she finally left. A light haze hung just above the road, veiling the imperfections of the town. The street lights glittered on the filmy air, and Amanda grinned at the fairy tale reflection.

"Finally."

She whirled around at the single word, blinking until she saw the tall, shadowy figure leaning against a car. Her hand clenched around the handlebar of her bike.

Doug ambled toward her, his long legs eating up the distance between them. "I was beginning to wonder if I had missed you, or if you were planning to spend the night in your office."

"I—I," she stammered and swallowed, trying again. "What are you doing here?"

He grinned and released her tight hold on the bicycle. He wheeled it toward his car and popped open the trunk, effortlessly picking up the bike and dropping it inside before slamming the lid down. Brushing his hands together, he just as effortlessly led her to the car and opened the passenger door.

Amanda froze, her hand gripping the roof of the car. "What are you doing?"

"Taking you home." He gently pried her fingers from the top of the car and then paused, her hand cradled within the larger grasp of his own hand. "You don't have other plans, do you?"

She shook her head, bemused by his authoritative air and how willingly her body responded to his command. Bob would say he had a powerful aura, she thought, probably from his years of working as a doctor.

As he bent down and fastened her seatbelt, she twisted her head and stared at him. She still couldn't understand why he was there. "How did you know I was still here? Most of the offices in the building have been deserted for hours."

His face was only inches away from hers and she could see the shadow of his beard on his cheek. Her breathing faltered, and she clutched the edge of her seatbelt, wondering if she needed more sleep, amazed that one single man could arouse such confused feelings in her.

He clicked the belt into place and straightened, leaning his arm along the top of the car and keeping his face at eye level. "I don't have supernatural powers, if that's what you're wondering. I heard the security guard ask someone he called Megan if you were still in the building."

She glanced at her watch. Megan had gone home almost two hours earlier. "You've been waiting for me that long?"

He shrugged and stood up, taking hold of her door. "You didn't want me to come into the office, and you didn't return my calls. Short of laying siege to your house, I didn't know how else I could make contact with you. Besides, it didn't seem like a good night for a bike ride."

She bit her lip as he walked around the car and climbed into his seat. As he started the engine, she shifted and noticed that this was a different car than the one he had been driving the night they visited her family.

"What happened to your other car?" she asked, determined to squash any thought that he had waited for her for any personal reason.

"One of the perks of being a car dealer—always a new vehicle to take home." He slowed down at the entrance to the office complex and then joined the late evening traffic with barely a break in the car's motion.

"The other one sold?"

He nodded, reaching down to shift gears. "And this one will probably go next."

Changing jobs, changing cars. Was that the way he took life? No commitments required, no regrets expressed when the time was over.

She wondered if he exchanged friends as easily. The thought of one day waking up and finding that Doug McCallister had moved on, leaving Coppertown for another job, another town, caused a lump in her throat. She swallowed, and the pain moved lower, lodging in the center of her stomach.

"Are you okay?" His fingers lightly brushed against her hand as he shifted for a turn.

His gentle words and the soft touch of his hand brought the pain back to her throat. She stared out of the window, noticing the way the fog almost hid the houses from sight, shrouding the town in a ghostly light.

Get a hold of yourself, she scolded silently. *You're just tired from working so hard.*

She blinked and forced her lips to curl in a smile before turning toward him. "I'm still a little surprised."

He braked quickly, his arm stretching in front of her and holding her into place. When the car in front turned, he moved his arm back to its place on the gearshift.

Her heart resumed its normal beating. *Why are you here?* she asked herself. *Why didn't you say you had to go home? You know what's going to happen.*

On the heels of these thoughts came another, almost blinding in its clarity: *But maybe this time things will work out.*

The misty air seeped into the car through his open window, mingling with the new car scent. *I'm asleep, this is a dream,* she thought. *I've been working too hard, and I fell asleep in the office. If I reach out, I'll touch my desk, the couch. . . .*

Her fingers brushed against his arm as he shifted the car. With a tiny squeak of alarm, she yanked her hand back and clenched them both in her lap, staring straight ahead at the foggy road.

From the corner of her eye, she saw him shift his head toward her. "Amanda, are you okay?"

She nodded. "I'm fine. I've just got a lot on my mind right now."

"The Willowton project?"

His low-voiced question calmed her. "Actually, I haven't spent much time on that project lately," she said in her natural voice. "Bob has been home with the flu, and Megan and I have been trying to keep up with the other contracts. Mark and Sierra have been working on the Willowton project, making plans for the fundraising dance and last-minute ad campaigns."

"Still going ahead with the dance, then?"

"We have to." She shifted in her seat, bringing one knee up, so that she could face him. Talk of her work always brought back her confidence, and she felt on safer ground. "If we wait until after the vote comes back, we won't be able to pull it off."

" 'Hope springs eternal,' " he quoted, and she chuckled.

"We have to believe in our product, or who else will?" she countered, and he acknowledged her comment with a slight dip of his head.

He signaled and pulled into an apartment complex. "What are we doing here?" she asked.

"My turn to cook dinner."

Her cheeks flushed as she thought of the fiasco from the other night. Then his words sunk in. "Your place?"

He nodded and slid the car easily into a parking place near a set of glass entry doors. "I thought since we can't make connection about the project at the workplace, we could try over dinner." He shut off the engine and grinned at her. "You do have dinner breaks, don't you?"

Slightly miffed that he thought she did nothing but work, she tilted her chin and looked down her nose at him. "Of course, I do. After all, I own the company."

His laughter echoed in her ears even after they left the car. He led the way up the three stairs to the lobby and smiled at the security guard before guiding her toward the bank of elevators with a gentle hand at her back.

At the fourth floor, she waited while he fitted his key into the lock and then clicked on the lights. She followed him down a narrow hallway that opened into a wide living room. A large picture window dominated the room, providing a full view of one of the many parks Coppertown boasted.

"How pretty!" Amanda headed straight for the window, leaning forward and picking out different landmarks. "I didn't even know this building existed."

Doug flicked the switch in the kitchen and opened the refrigerator. "They just built it last year. Dick was able to get me an apartment as soon as he heard I was interested in coming back."

She turned around, noting the sparse furnishings. A lone couch occupied the space in front of the fireplace, and three bar stools pulled up to the counter that separated the kitchen from the living room comprised the dining room. Only one shelf of the bookcase housed any books, and a single lamp lit the room in front of her.

Either he's just moved in, or he's not planning to stay long, she thought.

She crossed the room and perched on one of the bar stools. Unable to ask him about his future plans, she concentrated instead on his past. "Are you from here originally?"

He pulled out several containers and shook his head. "No, but my cousin's lived here all of his life. I used to visit him every summer and stay for a few weeks."

She picked up a piece of celery from the relish plate and nibbled on the end of it. "That's why you moved here, then?"

He twisted the temperature control on the oven and then popped a pan into it. "Not really. I mean, in a way I suppose Dick is the reason I moved here. He introduced me to Mary."

The celery suddenly tasted wooden, and Amanda chewed mechanically before she was able to swallow it and manage what she hoped sounded like an interested, "Oh?"

"She was the best friend of Dick's sister. At first we just thought the girls were pests and wouldn't have anything to do with them." He straightened up with a grin. "Probably the way your sisters used to treat you."

"I wasn't a pest!"

His grin widened, crinkling the corners of his dark eyes. "Should I ask them?"

She rested both hands on the counter, prepared to defend her honor, and then backed down under the gleam in his eyes. "Okay," she relented. "Maybe I was a nuisance some of the time. But that was just because they wouldn't let me do anything with them."

"That's what my aunt used to say." He tossed the already prepared salad, adding a vinaigrette dressing. "We finally believed her and found out she wasn't totally wrong. The girls could be fun company."

And then you married Mary, she thought, amazed at the turn in the conversation.

He seemed to read her thoughts. "Mary's father was a doctor, and I was just getting interested in medicine. I spent a lot of time at their house when I visited Dick and his family, and one thing led to another. We became engaged before I even left for college."

"I never had a childhood sweetheart," she said, picking up another piece of celery to give her something to hold. "I was always so much taller than the boys in my class, and then I was too busy working to pay for school."

He handed her a plate and a small dish of vegetable dip. "Not one?"

She added carrots and olives to her plate. "Nope," she said cheerfully. "I dated a few guys in college, but by then I was determined to finish my degree early and start my own business. I didn't have time for a relationship."

"And now?"

The soft question hung in the air. Amanda's hand froze inches above the plate, a carrot grasped tightly between her thumb and forefinger. Her eyes locked with his. His smile had disappeared, and his lips were drawn together as he watched her.

Without shifting his gaze, he carefully pried the carrot from her hand, dropping it with a tiny clink on the plate. His fingers slid between hers, lacing them together with an intimate gesture that caused shivers to spread from her hands to the rest of her body. She couldn't tear her gaze away from him, trapped by his question and something else that hovered between them.

"You didn't answer," he whispered, his breath floating toward her and landing like a soft caress on her cheek. "Are you still too busy for a relationship?"

Images of new cars, the stack of projects on her desk, and the lack of furnishings in his apartment flitted across her mind and then disappeared in the promise of his liquid gaze. She licked her lips and braced herself as his head lowered.

This kiss erased all memories of the earlier, angry one. His lips touched hers briefly, and then he lifted his head, his eyes searching hers. One corner of her mouth edged upward, and his fingers tightened around her hand before he lowered his head again, this time crushing her lips under his.

She didn't know how long they stood that way, the kiss deepening as they held hands across the counter. When he moved around the edge of the counter, she met him half-way, her arms sliding up his back while his circled her shoulders. He gently tipped her head until it rested against his shoulder, never once breaking the contact of their lips.

Her heart pounded as she absorbed the touch of his broad shoulders under her fingertips. The nubby material of his shirt molded to his muscles, and the soft whiskers on his cheek rubbed against her skin, solid reminders of the differences that existed between them and yet pulled them together.

His lips called her away from the tensions of the day, from the phone calls and lists of chores she still had to accomplish. The frustrations that earlier had seemed so important vanished as his hands caressed her back and danced across her shoulders, their touch as light as the fog surrounding the town.

When he lifted his head, she murmured and raised one hand, reluctant to be sent back to the world. He caught her hand and raised it to his lips, his eyes only half-open as he smiled at her. "I take it that means yes," he said huskily.

She blinked, trying to remember the question. He chuckled and pressed a feather-light kiss on her lips before running his knuckles down her cheek, smiling into her eyes with a look that caused her insides to puddle. "A relationship," he reminded her.

His words jolted her back to reality. "A relationship?"

"Amanda, you can't ignore what's happening between us."

She struggled upright and pulled herself out of his embrace. "We just met, Doug. We don't have a relationship." *We can't,* she thought frantically. *Not while you change cars as often as some people change socks. And your apartment doesn't have any furniture. And I can't cook, and I don't want to be dependent on anyone, even if your kisses make me forget my own name.*

The words screamed inside her head, but she couldn't phrase them. A cold, hard look replaced the warm expression in his eyes and he stepped backward. "I see." He bent down and opened the oven.

The pan he pulled out was covered with charred cheese, and he tossed it into the sink. Steam rose up with a menacing hiss. "At least our luck with dinner seems to be holding." He dropped the potholders on the counter with a disgusted look. "*I've* burnt the dinner this time."

"Maybe I should go." She chewed on her bottom lip, hoping he would try to dissuade her, hoping that he would take her back in his arms where she could think clearly again.

He nodded. "That's probably not a bad idea. I'm suddenly not in the mood to discuss your campaign plans."

He walked around her, and she silently followed him down the hallway. His back was ramrod straight, his arms at his sides. A tiny muscle throbbed in his jaw, but she couldn't tell if he was angry at her or at himself.

When he opened the door and stepped aside for her to pass him, she hesitated. "My bike?"

"Of course."

His tone was brisk and clinical; the professional without a moment to spare, squeezed out the charming man who had riddled her senses. She wanted to call him back, to enjoy whatever moments they had together, but the words stuck in her throat.

Outside, he didn't say anything, only opening the trunk and dragging her bicycle out. He waited while she snapped on her helmet and then slammed down the trunk.

"Good night," she said cautiously.

"Good night." He started toward the apartment building and then swung around. Her heart slowed. *Now,* she thought, *now he'll open his arms, and I can show him that I was confused, that I didn't know what he expected of me.*

His arms remained at his sides. "Be careful, Amanda. The fog's getting thicker, and you'll be hard to see in that dark jacket."

Her heart resumed its dull beating. "I know. I'll stay on the side streets."

He nodded. "Good night, then."

The light from the apartment building reflected on the reddish highlights of his hair, frosty in the swirling fog. She climbed on her bike and pedaled into the night, away from the uncertain promise of his kisses, afraid that she had tossed away something very precious without knowing what it was.

Chapter Nine

Amanda ran her hand through her short curls, leaning back in her chair with her eyes closed. She rubbed her temples as she talked. "Okay, the caterers are lined up; we have the florists coming in the afternoon to decorate the ballroom. . . ." She straightened up and stared at Bob. "The musicians? Have you confirmed the musicians?"

Bob nodded. "Last week, Amanda." He frowned. "What's the matter with you today? You don't usually get this anxious about one of our projects."

"I know, I know." She jumped to her feet and paced to the window, pulling back the curtain. A shiny blue sedan drove into the parking lot, and her breath caught in her throat. When a young woman with a small boy in tow climbed out, she turned back to Bob.

"I just don't feel right about this campaign. It's been almost a week, and we haven't heard a word from Mrs.

103

Carlson or her group. Not a letter to the editor or even a nasty ad. Nothing."

"Maybe she's changed her mind, and they're giving in," Bob suggested.

"No." Amanda paced around the room, her hands wrapped around her waist. "After that last phone call, she wouldn't give in so easily. She's probably waiting until the last minute for a concerted media blitz."

Bob shuffled the papers he held in his lap. "Don't worry about it, Amanda. The phone surveys show the community strongly in support of the community building."

She sat back down, her elbows on the desk and her fingers laced together. "I hope you're right. Otherwise we're going to have a lot of unnecessary expense."

After Bob left, she twirled her chair around and tipped back, staring out of the window. Bob and Megan both took the silence from Mrs. Carlson's camp as a positive sign, but she couldn't rid herself of the nagging feeling that it was just the calm before the storm. Mrs. Carlson had given all indications that she was determined to block the community building.

Amanda swung around and flipped open the top folder on her desk. Except for finalizing plans for the fundraiser dance, she had nothing left to do on the Willowton project. Their last two ads were running on the local news station, and Mark and Sierra had delivered the final newspaper ad that morning. In less than a week, she would know if their office had been successful, or if they would be part of the losing team.

After lunch, Megan came into the office to pick up a stack of folders that needed filing. The phone rang just as she reached the door. She raised an eyebrow and tried to shift the load to one hip.

"I'll get it," Amanda said, reaching for the phone.

"Thanks." Megan leaned against the door and waited while Amanda picked up the receiver.

"Blake Visions," Amanda said in her most professional voice.

"Amanda?"

Her hand tightened around the phone. Doug! She hadn't heard from him since the night she left his apartment. "Yes?"

"I know you didn't want me to call you at work, but this has to do with the Willowton project. I have someone who wants to meet you. He thinks he could help right now."

Her fingers relaxed their death grip on the phone. Megan still stood in the doorway, and Amanda waved her on. She waited until her secretary was out of sight before speaking. "How?"

"You have to see it to understand," Doug said.

She glanced at the daybook open on her desk. "I'm free this afternoon. Can they come to the office?"

"No, he thinks you need to see him in action."

Despite her confused feelings, his words intrigued her. "See him in action?"

Doug's soft chuckle sounded over the line. "He's a little bit of a character, but he's good-hearted. He thinks he might have an idea to help share the need for a community building. Can you get someone with a video camera for about three this afternoon?"

Mark wasn't available, but Bob was pretty handy with a camera. For the first time in the last several days, she felt her spirits rise. But she knew she had to proceed cautiously. "The vote is only a few days away. Isn't he stepping forward a little late?"

"This is the first they've met since the Carlson group started their park campaign." Doug hesitated. "I thought this might be helpful, but maybe you're right."

His tone erased all of her doubts. She couldn't let her personal feelings affect her professional life. The two areas had to stay separate. "No, you're right. It's not too late yet." She picked up a pencil. "Okay, where do we go?"

"Just be outside your office building at three o'clock. We'll go from there."

He hung up without even saying goodbye. Amanda dropped the phone into the cradle, amazed at the rush of emotion that flowed through her. Just hearing his voice had perked her up, shattering the tired, listless feeling she'd experienced for the last four days.

At first she had been certain that he would call her at the office; she jumped every time the phone rang. She didn't know what she would say to him. Her reaction at his apartment had been one of instinct, and fear of disrupting a life that moved smoothly.

As the days passed, she wondered if she had severed any hope of a relationship with him by her foolish actions. Twice she considered calling him, but she held back. What would she say? How could she explain that she didn't want a relationship because she might be hurt?

After hours of soul searching, she could see now that she had approached every relationship with the idea that it wouldn't work out. She hadn't given any of them a chance to succeed. Instead, she had refused to look beyond the surface of each of the men she had dated, choosing those flaws that would most annoy her and magnifying them ten times without once comparing them to the strengths the men had.

Doug's kisses had changed all that. She rested her elbows on the desk and leaned her chin on her hands. She could picture him at the dealership, that unruly lock of hair slipping over his forehead, his dark eyes bright as he tried to convince someone that they needed the car he was showing them.

She roused herself from the daydream and buzzed Bob's office. "Can you join me about 2:50 with the camera?"

"Yes. What's up?"

"I'm not sure. Something to do with the Willowton project."

By 2:30, she knew she would have to call it a day. Until she saw Doug again and knew what he thought about her, she wouldn't be able to concentrate on her work. She stacked the barely touched folders in a drawer and grabbed her backpack.

"So, what's the big deal?" Megan asked, swiveling around in her chair.

"I don't know." Amanda straightened the magazines on the table in the waiting area and nudged a potted plant into the middle of the file cabinet.

"Amanda, what's going on?"

Amanda swung around, her eyes wide. "What do you mean?"

"Whenever you start rearranging the office, something's going on." Megan wrinkled her brow, her hand on her chin.

"It's not something to do with this Doug McCallister guy, is it?"

Amanda shifted away from Megan's steady gaze, adjusting an aerial view of the town that hung on the wall. "Of course not. We're meeting him, but that's all. He's helping with the Willowton project, you know," she added with what she hoped was an innocent air.

"Okay, Amanda, I'm ready."

She grabbed Bob's arm as if he were a lifesaver. "Great." With a large smile, she waved gaily to Megan. "Hold the fort, Megan. I don't know when we'll be back."

She practically dragged Bob out of the office and toward the elevator. "What's the hurry?" he asked. "You said 2:50. It's not even 2:45."

She loosened her hold and he smoothed down the sleeve of his jacket. "I know. I just needed some fresh air. And you know if I'd stayed around the office, we'd get a phone call right at 2:50 that only I could handle. This way, Megan can truthfully say we're out of the office."

Bob squinted at her, and she waited for the inevitable aura comment. He studied her for a moment and then nodded. "You're right. Now, tell me what we're doing."

She gave him the same answer she'd given Megan. "I don't know for sure. We're going to see someone who thinks he can help swing the community to our side."

The elevator stopped at the main floor. Bob hefted the bag containing the video camera over his shoulder and picked up the tripod. "I think you're worrying needlessly, Amanda. I don't feel anything but a positive aura around this whole project."

She followed him down the hallway and into the sunshine. He leaned the tripod against the building and shifted the bag to the ground. "I hope your auras are right this now," she said. "I hate the thought of losing to someone like Mrs. Carlson."

"Maybe we should look at this from her viewpoint," Bob began diplomatically.

Amanda stared at him. "Bob, there's no reason Coppertown needs another park." She lifted her hands as he started to speak. "I know, I know. We're destroying the earth by tearing up the countryside and putting up buildings all over the place. But we're not tearing up the countryside here, Bob. The building is already there. If we use the existing building, we won't need to destroy any other land later when they finally decide they *do* want a community building."

"Effective argument," a deep voice said behind her.

She whirled around, her hand at her throat. Doug smiled at her. "Have you used that one recently?"

She nodded, unable to speak. He looked even better than she remembered. He didn't have his jacket on, and he'd unbuttoned the top two buttons of his ivory-colored shirt. The sunlight glinted on his dark hair, shooting red-gold sparks toward her.

He was smiling, his lips curved in his lopsided grin. Her own lips curved in response, and a delicious quiver started at the tip of her toes and moved rapidly up her spine.

"Amanda?"

"Mmmm?"

"Amanda!"

She broke contact with Doug at the insistent question in Bob's voice. "I'm sorry, Bob, what did you say?"

His eyebrows pulled together, and he stared at first Doug and then her. His eyes widened, and his mouth opened into a startled, "Oh!"

His reaction confused her. "Bob, are you okay?"

He nodded several times. "Amanda, I—I . . ." He held up one hand, pressing it toward the two of them.

"Is he okay?" Doug whispered in her ear.

She nodded, her eyes still on Bob. He was gasping for air, his hand waving around his face, his mouth still open. "I think he's getting some sort of reading," she whispered.

One corner of Doug's mouth lifted in a grin, but he didn't say anything. Amanda stepped forward and gently touched Bob's arm. "Bob?"

He snapped his mouth closed and bent over. He took a deep breath and exhaled slowly while he stood up. "I'm fine."

"What happened?" Amanda asked.

"I . . ." He stopped, glancing at Doug.

"Oh, Bob, this is Doug McCallister. Doug, this is Bob Owens, part of the staff at Blake Visions."

The two men shook hands, their eyes curious as they surveyed each other. Amanda watched, amused at the male ritual.

Satisfied by what he saw, Bob smiled at Amanda. "I just had the strangest feeling come over me."

"A reading?"

He frowned. "No. I never get those without a lot of preparation."

She hurried to smooth his ruffled feelings. "I'm sorry, I didn't realize that." She bent down and picked up the tripod. "Why don't you tell us what happened while we're on the way?"

Doug took the hint and led them to his car. This time he was driving a four-door dark green sedan, not unlike the car she had watched earlier that morning. She lifted one eyebrow when he opened the trunk for Bob's equipment.

His sigh rumbled through his chest, but his eyes twinkled. "Another sale," he said sadly.

She laughed. "And they've moved you into the big boys' cars, I see."

His laugh wrapped around her, warming her, isolating her from the rest of the world while they shared their own personal joke. "I know. No more schoolboys to convince they need a sports car. Now I have to deal with staid businessmen."

She quirked an eyebrow, and he raised one hand before slamming the trunk closed. "And businesswomen."

"Thank you."

Bob slid into the back seat before she had a chance to offer him the front seat. With her senses still attuned to the earlier private moment, she suddenly felt shy sitting next to Doug.

He rested his arm against the back of her seat while he backed out of the parking spot. His hand brushed the nape of her neck. He didn't lower his hand once he had cleared the row of cars, and even though she was tempted to lean into his comforting warmth, she held herself stiffly away from that seductive touch.

The seat rustled behind her, and she turned around quickly, grateful that Bob was with her. "Now tell me what happened out there."

Bob lifted his hands and shook his head. "I don't know. It wasn't like my usual feelings. Just a warm, comfortable glow, like I had stumbled into the middle of a cheerful family drama. You know, where the couples can pick up a thread of conversation even after they've been apart for a while."

Amanda tipped her head and ran a finger over the soft gray interior. "What about the Willowton project?" she asked quietly.

"Not a thing. That's what was so strange. I was sure that I would see a happy resolution, that Mr. McCallister would be the answer to our problems."

No, she thought, *he tends to bring new ones along.* Her finger circled the paisley design in the middle of the seat. She peeked through her lashes at Doug, but he was concentrating on his driving, both hands now holding the steering wheel.

She cleared her throat. "Are you going to tell us where we're going?" she asked Doug.

He shook his head. "No. He asked me not to give you any clues before we arrived."

"Not even a name?"

"Not even a name."

She leaned against the seat and watched the downtown change into a residential area. Near the junior high, neat rows of houses lined the street. Doug slid the car into the curb a block away from the brick building.

Amanda glanced at the modest white clapboard in front of them. "Here?"

"Here."

She climbed out of the car and waited on the sidewalk while Bob retrieved his equipment. She managed to keep up with Doug's long stride and could hear Bob wheezing behind her.

"What are we doing here?" he whispered.

"I don't know. We'll see in a minute."

A man Amanda guessed to be in his seventies opened the door at Doug's knock. "You made it." He clasped Doug around the shoulders and gave him a brief hug.

He leaned around Doug's broad shoulders. "You came. Good." He held the door open, a smile splitting the weathered skin of his face. "Come in, come in. We don't have much time to set up."

The door opened into a small living room. Chairs of all sizes and shapes cluttered every corner and every inch of space. Amanda squeezed between a large recliner and a Queen Anne chair and stood in a small, empty space in the middle of the room while she waited for Doug to introduce them.

"Put the camera in that corner," the older man instructed Bob. "You'll be out of the way there, but you can see everything."

Amanda perched on the edge of a straight-backed chair, so that Bob could move past her. While he fiddled with the camera, she sent a sharp look toward Doug.

"Harris, Miss Blake would like an introduction."

The older man stopped his fussing and leaped forward with amazing agility for a man his age. "Of course, of course, where are my manners? I don't really need an introduction to you, though, young lady."

Amanda gave him a puzzled look. "Have we met before?"

A grin creased his face, giving him the look of a mischievous leprechaun. "You were much younger and not exactly happy to see me. If I remember correctly, you burst into tears the first time we met."

She couldn't place the man at all. "I'm sorry, I don't remember this."

He cackled, rubbing his hands together. "Oh, Amanda, you're just like your mother. She was just that gullible, too. When I told her she was expecting triplets, and with your sisters and brother already at home, I thought she was going to faint."

A memory pierced her confusion. A man known as much for his sense of humor as his medical expertise. "Dr. Peterson."

He nodded. She smiled at the man who had brought her into the world and then kept track of her health for the next seven years. "I thought you moved away after you retired."

He nodded, hopped over a low stool, and sat on a rough-cut chair that resembled tree branches nailed together. "I did. But I missed my friends, and I didn't like the sun all of the time. So I moved back last year."

"And now?" She glanced at him and then over to Doug, hoping that one of them would explain why they were sitting in a crowded living room with her childhood doctor.

A commotion at the front door ended their conversation. "Doc, you won't believe what happened!" a youthful voice shouted before the owner came into the room.

He stopped at the edge of the room, his eyes narrowing in appreciation as he took in Amanda's appearance. "Hello, pretty lady."

"Manners, Matt," the doctor said softly.

The gleam of approval didn't leave the boy's eyes but he extended a hand politely. "Matt Towers."

She shook his hand and added her own name. Then she watched him rush over to the doctor's side. "Look at this," he said, handing the older man a piece of paper.

Dr. Peterson studied the paper carefully and then lifted his head with a grin. "You did it, Matt."

"I sure did. And all thanks to you." The tall, lanky teen slung his backpack to the floor and plopped down on a chair.

Dr. Peterson shook his head. "No, it was your hard work." He tipped his head toward Amanda and Doug. "Mind if we share your good news?"

Matt's grin revealed a strong set of white teeth. "Not a bit."

The paper the doctor handed her sported a large "B" at the top of it. "Matt had a science test yesterday," Dr. Peterson explained. "We've been waiting for his grade."

"That's good," Amanda said cautiously.

Matt's grin widened. "It's great. Last semester, I almost flunked out of school." He dropped his hand on the older man's shoulder and gave it a squeeze. "This man gave me another chance."

Amanda watched as three more teens invaded the small room, their large bodies dropping into chairs while their loud voices reverberated against the walls. As they exclaimed over the news that one of their group had been chosen for a school play, she leaned over to Doug. "What's going on here?" she whispered.

"Harris felt a little useless in his retirement and wandered into the junior high one day last fall. He heard Todd there," he motioned to a skinny redhead wearing a bandana wrapped around his forehead, "use a few foul words just before he was suspended from school. Since Harris helped deliver the principal, he thought he'd find out what was going on."

"And?" Amanda prompted when Doug stopped speaking.

"He found out there are a lot of kids in this community who need somebody to care about them."

"Their parents?"

"These boys are luckier than most. Their parents *do* care about them, but they just don't have time to give them the attention they need. Most of them live with a single mother who's trying to keep food on the table."

A loud laugh echoed around the room, and Amanda looked up to see one of the boys flushed with color. "And why not?" he asked, his hands on his hips. He glared at the others but instead of making them back down, they hooted even louder.

"Josh is going to play a teacher in the school play," Dr. Peterson explained to Amanda and Doug.

"He deserves a class full of kids just like us," the fourth boy guffawed.

The other boys sobered, shaking their heads. "Like we *used* to be," Todd retorted.

The other boy lifted his head as if struck. "Yeah, like we used to be." He scrambled in his bag and pulled out a book. "Look at this, Doc, the teacher thought I might like to find out more about Germany, since that's where my dad is."

"A serviceman," Doug whispered. "Since he never married Aaron's mom, she didn't go with him."

They spent another half hour with the group; Bob's camera went unnoticed in the corner. Dr. Peterson offered them refreshments before they left, but Amanda declined. "Your boys need you," she said, pressing his hand warmly. "And if I'm going to use this tape before the election, we need to edit as soon as possible."

Bob packed up his gear and sidled up to Amanda. "We can't use the boys' pictures unless we have release forms," he murmured.

"You're right." She chewed on her lower lip. "Do you have any with you?"

He dug into the camera bag and pulled out a stack of sheets. Shuffling through them, he finally extracted four wrinkled forms.

"But will anyone sign these?" Amanda asked.

Doug nodded. "Their parents are thrilled about what's happened to their sons since they met Harris." He waved the forms in the air until he had the boys' attention. "You know about the community building being proposed for the old Willowton house?"

The boys nodded. "Miss Blake," Doug said, nodding toward Amanda, "is trying to make that happen. Dr. Peterson invited us to visit this afternoon, so that she could get some pictures of you to use in the campaign."

"We're going to be in the paper?" Todd asked.

She smiled at him. "No, actually we were shooting some film that I think will work for a television spot."

"We're going to be TV stars?" Matt's dark eyes widened.

"Maybe not stars, but you will be on television."

He hooked his thumbs in the belt loops of his jeans. "Hey, Josh, you're not the only famous actor in this room."

Amanda chuckled at his antics. "But you can only be in the spot if we have a release form." She indicated the papers Doug held. "Can you have your parents sign them tonight and bring them over to Dr. Peterson tomorrow afternoon?"

"Sure." "Yeah." "Of course."

Doug handed out the papers and a few minutes later, he shepherded Amanda and Bob out of the small house amid invitations to come again. Amanda assured them she would be happy to do so.

Once in the car, she leaned against the seat and cupped her chin with her hand. "I haven't seen Dr. Peterson in years. He looks great."

"Working with those boys has given him a new lease on life," Doug said. "He's always drumming up more support from the people he knows."

"Well, he should find a lot of help." She grinned at Doug. "He delivered half of the town."

"My sister was the first baby he ever delivered," Bob's voice chimed in from the back.

Amanda twisted around. "Really?"

Bob nodded his head vehemently. "Yes. And she was a holy terror when we were growing up. It's a good thing I saw what he was doing before he asked us for help. I'm not sure I would have agreed since he saddled me with Beth."

Bob's unexpected outburst startled a snicker out of Amanda, and she was soon joined by both Doug and Bob. Their laughter stayed with them during the rest of the drive to the office.

Chapter Ten

Only a few scattered cars sat in the parking lot. Amanda held the tripod while Bob picked up the camera bag. "I'll take this upstairs," she told him. "You can go on home."

"What about editing the tape?"

"We'll come up with a voice-over and lead-ins tomorrow," she said. He gave her a mulish look. "If you feel guilty about leaving, you can draw up some ideas about what would work best."

He didn't relinquish the bag. "I'll carry this upstairs for you. You don't need to carry everything."

"I'll take it." Doug reached over and plucked the bag from Bob's hands.

Bob smiled at the younger man and released the bag. "I'll see you in the morning, then, Amanda. It was nice meeting you, Doug."

He whistled as he headed toward the back of the lot. "I

can carry both of them," Amanda insisted, reaching for the shoulder strap of the bag.

Doug swung it out of reach. "I'll carry it." He rubbed his free hand over his chin. "Amanda, about the other night . . ."

"No, it's okay, I should apologize," she inserted quickly.

"Apologize?"

She nodded. "I—well—it was just a kiss."

"I know and it was my fault. We were just going to be friends, and I was way out of line. It won't happen again." He stuck out his hand. "Deal?"

Her hand moved slowly toward his. When her fingers touched the rough edges of his hand, he grasped her hand tightly and shook it once before releasing her.

A feeling of emptiness washed over her. What was the matter with her? This was what she wanted. She'd spent five days worrying needlessly. He hadn't been upset because she'd overreacted to his kiss. He seemed more than willing to put the episode behind them and remain friends.

She wrenched open the building door and stomped toward the elevators.

"Good evening, Miss Blake." The security guard smiled at her.

"Good evening." She nodded her head toward Doug. "He'll be back as soon as he helps me get this up to the office."

In the elevator, she kept her face deliberately averted from Doug. Just before she exited on her floor, he blocked her way with a strong arm across the door and his foot propping it open. "What's the matter with you?"

"Nothing. Now if you don't mind, I need to find out what I missed this afternoon."

"Amanda."

She lifted her chin and faced him squarely. "You want to be just friends? Fine. Now as one friend to another, will you let me by so I can get to my office?"

He dropped his arm, his face twisted in amazement. She quickly slipped past him.

His footsteps echoed in the empty hallway. "You're mad because I want to be friends? I thought that was your decision."

"You're the one who didn't want to get involved," she flung over her shoulder. Her office key stuck and she slapped the door in frustration.

"Amanda." Tears pricked the back of her eyelids at his gentle tone. What *was* the matter with her? This was what she wanted, wasn't it?

He reached around her and gently eased her hand away from the key. The door sprung open under his touch.

"Even the key," she muttered.

Inside the office, she leaned the tripod against the wall and reached for the camera bag. Doug dropped it on a chair and stepped toward her.

She backed up until she felt the wall against her shoulders. "Amanda, we need to talk."

Trapped by his body, his breath mingling with her own, she shook her head and ducked to get away from him. "No, we don't."

The words left her mouth, and she blinked. Instead of Doug's face, a long line of men appeared in front of her eyes. It was happening again. She was protecting herself by squelching any hope of a relationship before she had a chance to get hurt.

Only this time it's too late, she thought sadly. *He already has the power to hurt me.*

"Amanda, I thought we were friends."

He placed his hands on either side of her face, stopping her escape. He lowered his head until it was only inches away from her. "Amanda, I don't know what you want from me. All I know is that, right now, all I can offer is friendship."

At his words, a tiny seed took root and raised its head out of the dark recesses of her mind. She tried to tuck it back away, but it was too strong. *I want more from you!* it shouted. *More than friendship, more than you're willing to give, and maybe more than I'm willing to take.*

As if he read her mind and could see the dawning awareness within her, he moved back slowly. "I've quit my job at the dealership," he said quietly. "I told Dick I'd stay through the month, and then I'm done."

"What are you going to do?"

He shook his head. "I don't know for sure. I have a few leads I'm following. I just know I'm not cut out to be a salesman."

"Would you be a doctor again?"

"I can't, Amanda. That part of my life is through."

"Are you moving away?"

He didn't answer. A spasm shook her from head to toe, and she clamped her teeth together. After several silent moments, she gestured toward the door. "I appreciate your help with the equipment," she said in a flat, emotionless tone. "Maybe I'll see you sometime before you leave."

"Amanda, I don't want to leave like this."

"No?" Goaded beyond measure, afraid of the feelings that were taking form, she welcomed the anger that welled up inside. She plunked her clenched fists on her hips. "Doug, things happen to people all of the time. Bad things that they have to overcome. How you respond is your own choice." She gave a weary sigh and pointed to the door again. "I really need to work tonight. The vote is next Tuesday, and I have some last minute items to go over."

He nodded and walked toward the door. His hand on the knob, he turned toward her. "I'd like to see you again. I meant that about being friends."

She shrugged. "Well, maybe when you decide what you want to be when you grow up, you can look me up. I'll probably still be here."

The door swung shut. She leaned against the wall, suddenly exhausted. At the sound of the elevator's doors whirring open, the tears that had threatened during their encounter slid down her cheeks.

She dashed them away angrily. "I don't need him." She grabbed the camera equipment and lugged it into the back room before settling at her desk.

The top note was circled in red. "Mrs. Carlson called twice," Megan wrote. "She wants to set up a meeting time for tomorrow morning."

"Great." Amanda tapped her fingernail against the rest of the messages. In her current frame of mind, she was in no mood to discuss issues rationally with anyone. It was the perfect time to confront the illogical arguments of Mrs. Carlson.

Megan had added a personal note at the bottom of the message. "I found Rory's address and phone number. They're on the back."

Amanda flipped over the note. The sight of the Washington address and phone number cheered her. Dragging the phone forward, she quickly dialed the ten digits.

While she talked to Megan's friend, she jotted down notes. "I don't want this to be negative," she explained to the woman on the other end. "But your name alone could make a big difference in our campaign."

"I haven't seen my mother in years," Rory said. "We didn't part on the best of terms."

Amanda experienced a qualm of conscience. "If you would rather not . . ." she began.

"No, no. I think you're absolutely right. A community building would be an asset to Coppertown. By all means, use my name and picture if it will help."

Amanda spent the next several minutes fielding questions about the town. Rory gave the impression that she was starved for hometown news, and Amanda willingly gave her all the details she requested.

"If you do see my mother," Rory said in a quieter voice, "let her know I'm fine, and that the girls are enjoying school this year."

When she hung up, Amanda stared at the silent phone. Even though her mother and siblings often drove her crazy, how would she survive without knowing they were behind her?

She scanned the rest of the notes and then left the office. Outside the building, she glanced around, half hoping that Doug was regretting the earlier scene and waiting for her.

An empty parking lot greeted her, and she pedaled home to her empty house.

The next morning, she telephoned Megan to tell her that she would be in later. She stopped at the newspaper office. "Mrs. Carlson doesn't have any ads running this weekend, does she?" she asked the weekend editor at the end of their meeting.

The editor grinned. "Amanda, you know I can't tell you that."

She laughed and stood up. "It was worth a try. I thought maybe I'd just catch you off guard."

He escorted her to the door. "I've been in the newspaper business too long to be caught off guard." He held the door open. "Things will work out, you'll see. The people in town are too smart to be fooled by a smooth talker without substance."

She hoped he was right. She remembered several other votes that had produced results opposite from those expected. Surely this time wouldn't be one of those.

Megan was on the phone when she arrived at the office, and she grimaced and waved her hands at Amanda. Amanda gave her a puzzled look and waved back before pushing her bike down the hall. Her backpack over one shoulder, she opened the door of her office.

A woman dressed in a light blue wool-blend suit rose to her feet from the chair in front of Amanda's desk. She waited while Amanda advanced into the room.

Amanda glanced over her shoulder, wondering why Megan let someone into her office while she was gone. She turned her attention back to the woman and motioned to the chair. "Please, sit down."

She hung her backpack on the coat rack and took her seat behind the desk. "Did we have an appointment?"

"Your secretary said she informed you of my desire to meet."

The formal tone, delivered in a harsh voice, identified the woman confronting her. "Mrs. Carlson?"

"Yes." She folded her hands in her lap. "I think you'll find it's in your best interest to talk with me."

Amanda settled back in her chair, trying to give the impression that she was not threatened by the small, forceful woman in front of her. Mrs. Carlson was at least a foot shorter than Amanda but packed a lot of power in her small stature. The older woman exuded the image of a woman used to getting her own way. And as Amanda knew from her conversations with Megan and Rory, she didn't always consider the costs.

The thought of Rory bolstered Amanda's courage. "Of course, Mrs. Carlson, I'll be happy to talk with you. What would you like to discuss?"

Mrs. Carlson's eyes narrowed suspiciously. Amanda met the look with a cool smile that didn't reach her eyes. "I know you think I'm just an old-fashioned woman trying to stop things from changing. But children belong home with their parents, not gathering for trouble at a community building."

"And what if they don't have parents at home?" Amanda countered.

"Then that's the family's problem. We can't solve everyone's problems, Miss Blake. My husband and I have been married for over thirty years, and we've raised two daughters without the help of anyone else."

Amanda bit her tongue. She wasn't ready to divulge her trump card until she knew Mrs. Carlson's angle.

Mrs. Carlson unsnapped her purse and pulled out a fat envelope. "I realize this campaign is important to you," she said softly. She unfolded several sheets of paper with a picture attached. "How far are you prepared to go?"

She laid the pages on Amanda's desk and scooted it toward her with a well-manicured nail. Frowning, Amanda picked it up and stared into Doug's handsome face. "What is this?"

"Read it."

At the end of the first sentence, Amanda's blood froze in her veins. "This isn't true! It's all a pack of lies. He wasn't even there."

"You'll notice that we don't actually accuse Dr. McCallister of killing his wife. We just allude to the fact that the good doctor was unable to save his own wife and child."

Amanda dropped the filthy slurs on her desk. "Why are you doing this? He's not even involved in the campaign."

"But you're involved with him," Mrs. Carlson said softly.

Relief flooded through her, and she actually grinned, feeling better than she had since entering the room to find Mrs. Carlson seated in her office. "Your source is misinformed. Dr. McCallister and I are *not* involved."

Mrs. Carlson's finely arched brows contracted. "You've been seen around town with him."

"Perhaps. But I've been seen around town with a lot of different people. That doesn't mean I'm involved with any of them."

"It doesn't matter." Mrs. Carlson resumed her brisk demeanor. "You seem to be a caring person," she sniffed as if this was a weakness. "If you don't want these damaging articles printed, you'll stop your support of the community building and explain you've reversed your position."

Amanda's smile disappeared. She leaned forward, her palms lightly resting on the edge of her desk, belying the surge of anger coursing through her. "Mrs. Carlson, I will not reverse my position. I stand fully in support of the community building, and I believe the majority of the townspeople do, too. In fact, I believe that a number of former residents would also support the project, including your own daughter."

Mrs. Carlson didn't flinch. "My daughter?"

Amanda nodded, watching her opponent carefully. "Rory is more than happy to let us use her name and picture in a full-page ad that will run in Sunday's paper. While she recognizes she can't vote, she thought that knowing she supported the project might help our side."

"I see." Mrs. Carlson stood up and smoothed down the pristine lines of her skirt. "I may have underestimated you, Miss Blake. But I'm not prepared to admit defeat yet."

"I don't expect you to." Amanda stood up, but she didn't move around her desk. "I believe you can find your own way out."

She waited until the woman disappeared around the corner of the hall before slumping into her chair. A few moments later, Megan dashed into the room. "Are you okay? I tried to warn you."

Amanda nodded. "I know, I know. But nothing could have prepared me for her." She shook her head, reliving the confrontation. "She's mean, Megan, nasty. Not a speck of warmth in her. She didn't even budge when I said Rory would support us."

"Rory's going to support the project?"

"I called her last night." Amanda shifted, and the picture of Doug caught her eye. She groaned.

Megan darted forward. "What is it?"

"This." She handed the article to her secretary.

Megan read through the entire three pages before lifting anguished eyes to Amanda. "She's not going to publish this, is she? She'll run him right back out of town."

"I know it." Amanda bit her lip. She had to think, plan exactly how she would counter the threats presented by the articles. She couldn't let Mrs. Carlson print those damaging reports about Doug, but she wouldn't be blackmailed.

"What are you going to do?" Megan asked.

"I don't know. I thought she would back down once she heard about Rory. She said she underestimated me, and I think I did the same thing. She's a tough cookie."

The phone rang, and Megan returned to her responsibilities. Amanda tapped her fingers together, concentrating on the project and looking for creative solutions. Her best ideas usually leapt out when she least expected them, and she hoped one would spring forth soon.

By lunchtime, she still didn't have an inkling of an idea. For the first time, she wondered if Mrs. Carlson's interest in the park might be something more than a personal value choice. She almost discarded the thought of financial gain until she remembered something from the last ad the Carlson group had run in the paper.

She found the ads in her Willowton file. Near the bottom, they listed their sponsors, including the words "Carlson Contractors/Demolitions."

She looked the number up in the phone book. When the secretary answered, Amanda asked, "If I wanted a building demolished, how would I go about it?"

The young woman explained that the owners would be required to empty the building of any furniture or other items that they wanted. "Sometimes an auction might be held a few days before the demolition," she added.

"And what about everything else?"

"Usually we ask for rights to any of the fixtures, etc. remaining in the building. After the building is demolished, we'll haul off all of the debris and smooth over the property before we're finished."

She quoted Amanda several prices, stating that they would need to survey the property before they could give her a definite bid.

"I understand," Amanda said. "This will get me started. Thank you."

She hung up the phone, her brow furrowed in thought. From the young woman's information, most of the valuable furnishings would be gone before the demolition crew even arrived.

It just doesn't make any sense, she thought. Maybe Mrs. Carlson really just hates the thought of a community building.

The Willowton house sat in a wooded development in an older part of town. Amanda rode her bike in that direction after she left the office, coasting to a stop in front of the property. A once tall, proud building, the three-story building now looked neglected. Broken windows surrounded the lofty front door, and shingles were missing from the roof.

"Doesn't look very promising, does it?" an elderly gentleman walking his dog asked her.

She shifted her weight and leaned her foot against the curb. "No. But once the vote passes, she'll look like new again."

"Until all the kids start arriving." He tugged on the small poodle sniffing Amanda's foot.

She bent down and scratched behind the dog's ears. "The kids?"

"Hmmhmm." The man relaxed his hold on the dog, and she licked Amanda's hand. "They'll be here all hours, having parties, throwing trash, messing up the neighborhood."

"I don't think it will be that kind of a building," Amanda offered tentatively.

"They may say it won't be, but you just wait and see. Before you know it, we'll be afraid to go out of our homes. We'd be better off just knocking the old place down and building a park. At least nobody bothers with those anymore. Too busy watching television." The man's hand jerked on the dog's leash as he walked off, and she yipped.

Amanda gave the dog a sympathetic look. She hoped he was just talk and didn't take his frustration out on the dog. As she pedaled home, she wondered if the answer to Mrs. Carlson's opposition could be as simple as the one she had just been given.

She couldn't find a listing for the Carlsons in the phone book, but Megan still knew it by heart. "Used to spend as much time as I could there," she said when Amanda reached her. "I hated to be around Mrs. Carlson, but it was the only way I could see Rory. And for some reason, Mrs. Carlson didn't mind how much time I was there, since it kept Rory home."

"Megan, you know where the Willowton property is, don't you?" Amanda asked, breaking into her friend's reminiscences.

"Sure, I used to drive past it whenever I went to Rory's house." A long gasp fluted over the line. "Amanda, you don't think . . . ?"

Amanda nodded, even though Megan couldn't see her. "I think we've been making this too difficult for ourselves. Mrs. Carlson isn't against the community building because she's worried about the values of the family or even for financial reasons. She just doesn't want it to be in her neighborhood."

Chapter Eleven

Megan arrived at the office only minutes after Amanda did the next morning. "So, what are you going to do?" she asked breathlessly, shedding her fringed jacket.

Amanda typed a print command on the computer before answering. "About what?"

"Amanda! About Mrs. Carlson, what else?"

The printer stopped, and Amanda detached the paper, handing it to her secretary. "How does that sound?"

Megan skimmed through the five paragraphs and grinned. "Perfect. Are you going to use it Sunday morning?"

Amanda tucked her bike helmet under her arm and retrieved the paper from Megan. "I thought I would run it Monday morning. It all depends on what Mrs. Carlson decides to run tomorrow."

A soft spring sun warmed her as she pedaled the few blocks to Mrs. Carlson's house. Tall columns accented the colonial style of the house and a wrap-around porch invited visitors to sit and visit for a while. Of course, once they met Mrs. Carlson, they wouldn't stay long, Amanda thought, before she approached the huge front door.

The doorbell chimed throughout the house, and a white-aproned maid opened the door. "May I help you?"

"I'd like to see Mrs. Carlson, please," Amanda stated.

"Is she expecting you?"

She probably expects me to arrive with my tail between my legs, Amanda thought. She smiled at the maid. "She'll want to see me," she said softly. "Amanda Blake."

The woman opened the door a few inches farther, and Amanda stepped inside. Marble tile in a black and white pattern lined the floor, and a broad staircase rose up to the next level. Several doors opened off the entryway. Landscape paintings filled the spaces on the walls between the doors.

A door near the end of the hall opened, and Mrs. Carlson walked toward Amanda. "Miss Blake, I'm surprised to see you."

"Are you really?" Amanda asked softly.

A tiny crack appeared near the left corner of Mrs. Carlson's mouth, and Amanda wondered if she was seeing the beginning of a smile. The thought disappeared with the older woman's next words. "You're retracting your support?"

"No." She opened her backpack and took out the paper she had typed that morning. "In fact, I've prepared an ad to run Monday morning. I thought you might like to see it before it goes to print." She handed the sheet to Mrs. Carlson.

The woman scanned the pages and glared at Amanda. "You can't print this!"

"Why not? Is there anything there that isn't true?" Amanda asked with a bland tone.

Mrs. Carlson waved the paper at her. "This is nothing but a bunch of half-truths. If you print this, I won't be able to show my face in town again."

"But Mrs. Carlson, it is true that your husband takes a lot of trips with his secretary. And you have lost contact with your daughters. Why, do you even know how your granddaughters are doing in school?" Amanda paused and then added smoothly, "Rory says they're doing just fine, by the way."

"My family life is fine," Mrs. Carlson snapped. "We don't need anyone telling us what to do. We certainly wouldn't need a psychologist interfering."

"We don't say that you are seeing a psychologist. We just imply that perhaps family counseling would be helpful." Again Amanda paused, judging the reaction of Mrs. Carlson. "Of course, we may not run this ad at all. Instead, we might raise the question of whether or not you'll be putting this lovely house on the market if the community building proposal does pass."

Mrs. Carlson frowned. "Why would we sell our house?"

"Because you don't want to live near the community building. You don't care about family values or even the community. You just want to keep your little neighborhood free of anything or anyone who doesn't fit your stereotype of a perfect person."

"That's not true," Mrs. Carlson said, but her voice lacked conviction.

"It is true." Amanda zipped her backpack closed and slung it over her shoulder. "You're afraid of what might happen to your neighborhood if the proposal passes. And with your negative thinking, you're certain nothing good could possibly occur. But you didn't want anyone to know what you were really like. Instead, you spouted platitudes about family life while your own can't bear investigation."

She headed for the front door and stopped, glancing over her shoulder at the woman standing alone in the huge entryway. "I'd feel sorry for you, Mrs. Carlson, but I know you wouldn't appreciate it. You have more than most people even dream about, and yet you're still not happy. Oh, and just in case you *are* interested, your eldest granddaughter played Cinderella in the school play. Rory said she was an absolutely beautiful princess."

She welcomed the warmth of the sun after the chilly scene inside the house. Hopping on her bike, she pedaled as quickly as possible away from the elegant house and its unhappy inhabitants.

"What did she say?" Megan asked when Amanda arrived back at the office.

"Not much." Amanda dropped onto the couch. "I handed her the paper, made my feelings clear, and left. It's up to her now."

Sunday morning, Amanda dashed out to the driveway in her bare feet to retrieve the paper. She flipped through the pages carefully, searching for Mrs. Carlson's retaliation and the accusations that would send Doug out of town for good.

She reached the end of the paper and stared at it in surprise. Not a single ad bore the name of the Carlson group.

She had hoped that Mrs. Carlson would back down, but she hadn't expected a complete capitulation.

She went through the paper again, running her finger up and down each column. An editorial from the weekend editor discussed the positive aspects of the community building and urged the citizens to vote on Tuesday. Her ad filled half a page near the back of the first section and the next page listed polling places. The rest of the paper included the usual articles of both local and global interest.

"Nothing." A strange letdown feeling swept over her.

She laughed at her foolishness. "This is what you wanted," she said out loud. "Whether she supports the issue or not, at least she's withdrawn her opposition."

Monday morning, Megan brought in a huge bouquet of spring flowers and set them on Amanda's desk "For you, boss. You did it."

Amanda accepted the flowers but refused to take full credit for their success. "And we don't know for sure that we've won," she cautioned Megan and Bob, who had followed her into the office.

"What do you think?" Megan asked Bob. "Can you get a reading?"

He grimaced and closed his eyes for a few seconds. When he opened them, he nodded. "The Willowton project will do fine. I'm a little worried about you, though, Amanda."

"Me? If this project gets approved, we'll be swamped with clients. Why should you worry about me?"

A crease appeared between his bushy eyebrows. "You're not happy. The change that was going to take place, something's affecting it. And you need this change, Amanda, it's important for your future well-being."

An image of Doug's face bending to kiss her flashed into her mind. She brushed the tantalizing picture away. "We don't have time for readings, Bob. The fundraiser is Friday night, and we have other accounts."

Bob opened his mouth and snapped it shut at her look. "We have work to do," she reminded him.

On Tuesday night, they waited for the final results at the courthouse. The community building received overwhelming support. Amanda accepted the thanks of everyone gathered around her, but the victory seemed bittersweet.

"We did it!" Megan crowed, hugging Amanda tightly.

"We did. Now we just have to get enough funds to get the programs started and keep it going."

Megan leaned back, fixing Amanda with a frustrated look. "What's the matter with you? You're acting like a wet blanket."

Amanda rubbed her hand over her eyes. "I'm sorry, Megan. I think all the excitement of the last few weeks has just worn me out. I'll be fine after a good night's sleep."

"Well, you deserve one." Megan hugged her again. "Go home, get some rest. Come in late tomorrow. I can take care of anything that comes up."

"I just might do that."

She pedaled home through the quiet night. The other issues on the ballot had been routine, and except for the small group waiting at the courthouse, no one else seemed particularly excited about the results. A slight breeze blew across her neck and rustled the leaves of the trees.

An owl hooted overhead. A half moon shone down on her, and she rode over the shadows it threw on the earth.

This is all I need, she thought as she neared her street. The promise of a hot bath, a good book. I don't need someone waiting for me at home, wondering when I'll be back.

She rolled the bike into the shed. Her feet crunched on the driveway and she pulled out her house keys. As she climbed the steps, she could imagine Doug sitting beside her, talking about his wife and how much she meant to him, how he couldn't forget her and move into a new relationship. *I bet his memories don't keep him warm at night,* she thought, unlocking the door.

The phone rang, and she picked it up after the third ring. "Hello."

"Amanda, congratulations!"

"Hi, Mom. Yeah, it is good news. It seems kind of strange after all our work that it's over, though. I think I liked the anticipation more than the actual win."

Her mother chuckled. "Oh, Amanda, it's not over. You have the fundraising dance on Friday."

Amanda kicked off her shoes and curled up on the couch. Her mother's voice relieved the emptiness of her house. They chatted about the plans for the dance for several minutes, and then her mother shocked her with a comment about Doug eating dinner with them.

"Doug was at your house?"

"Yes. Your father saw him at the car dealership and invited him over. He's a darling man, and we had a wonderful visit."

"What was Dad doing at the dealership?"

"Looking for a car," her mother replied. "He's been talking about trading in the sedan for several weeks now."

Amanda's eyes narrowed suspiciously. Her father's car was barely a year old, and he spent every Saturday washing and polishing it. "Mom."

"Oh, dear," her mother said. "Look at the time. I need to go, honey, and you need your sleep. You've got a big week ahead of you."

Her bath forgotten, Amanda wandered into her bedroom. Why had Doug gone to her parents' house? If he was intent on leaving at the end of the month, would he think about forging new friendships? Had he decided to stay?

"He has to eat, Amanda," she scolded herself. "Just because he has dinner with your parents doesn't mean he's changed his plans."

The question of why he had gone to her parents' house nagged her during the last-minute preparations for the fundraiser dinner. Megan screened her calls during the next two days, only putting through the ones that directly related to the event on Friday night. Mark and Sierra spent more time in the office, dealing with the other accounts, while Bob directed all of his energies to helping Amanda, and in the process, kept her on the brink of running away.

"He's driving me crazy," she muttered to Megan on Friday morning. The florist had arrived at the hotel ballroom, and they were watching his assistants arrange the hundreds of blooms.

"Bob means well," Megan said.

Amanda gave her an incredulous look. "Last week you were ready to strangle him."

"That was last week." She patted Amanda's arm. "He's concerned about you, that's all. You mean a lot to all of us."

Touched by the simple words, Amanda nevertheless felt compelled to explain her feelings. "He keeps talking about this dance and how it's going to change my life. Right now, I just want it to be over."

"Everything will be fine. You're probably the most organized person I know. That's why your business is so successful."

Mollified by the praise, Amanda smiled. "It is going to be okay, isn't it?"

"Yes." She pushed Amanda toward the door. "Now go home and take a long bath, put on that sexy dress you bought, and come back ready to party."

"I'm supposed to be the boss," Amanda grumbled, "and yet everyone's always telling me what to do."

Megan grinned. "That's because you take care of everybody else, and you're always forgetting about yourself."

Pedaling home, Amanda wondered if that was true. Did she ignore herself? She didn't think so. She went to the movies, she relaxed with a good book more nights than she didn't, she exercised, ate right. What more did she need?

Someone to share all of this with, she thought. Being with Doug had shown her exactly why her parents and siblings raved about the marital state. She had enjoyed catching his eye when they were at Dr. Peterson's house and whispering about his program with the boys. She liked discussing the issues with him, hearing his opinion and expressing her own ideas with someone who really wanted to listen.

And she liked being held in arms that met her halfway, that shielded her from the cold and reminded her that life could go on. When Doug held her, her problems melted away, and even though she knew they didn't go away completely, she felt strengthened by his concern and able to confront them head on.

By the time she arrived back at the hotel, she was a bundle of nerves. Her bath hadn't relaxed her. Her thoughts had continued to revolve around Doug, wishing that he was picking her up instead of the cab she had ordered.

She pressed her hands against her stomach and inhaled. She exhaled the breath slowly, closing her eyes and focusing on positive images. She felt a little calmer when she walked into the still empty ballroom.

"Amanda, now don't panic," Megan said, vibrant in a gold lamé dress that showed off her back and slender neck.

"Megan, if there's a problem, just tell me straight out," Amanda ordered. "I won't panic unless you keep the news from me any longer."

"Well, one of the catering trucks had a slight accident on the way over here."

Amanda clutched Megan's hands. "Megan, all of it. Now."

"Most of the food is here," Megan said. "But the desserts are a little mangled."

"How mangled?"

"As in, you won't know what you're eating or which side is up."

Amanda groaned and then took another deep breath. "Okay, this will be fine." She headed toward the back of the ballroom and the kitchen doors.

The caterer lifted her head from a tray of unidentifiable objects. "Oh, Amanda, I'm so sorry." She scowled at a young man hovering near the back of the room. "He took the curve near the high school a little too fast."

"How bad is it?" Amanda asked, surveying the neat trays of hors d'oeuvres that she could see. Megan was right. The rest of the food looked wonderful.

"I think I can salvage most of them." She separated two blobs of what appeared to be miniature cheesecakes. "People are usually so busy talking during these kind of evenings that they don't really look at what they're eating. And they still taste fine."

"I appreciate whatever you can do, Cindy."

Amanda returned to the ballroom. The musicians had arrived and were warming up in the alcove set aside for them. Waiters circled the room, lighting candles and straightening chairs.

Her parents were among the first to arrive. "It looks beautiful," Patricia gushed.

Amanda smiled at her. "So do you, Mom. That dress is gorgeous."

Her mother spun around, the full skirt of her midnight blue evening gown billowing around her still trim figure. "Your father would die if he saw the bill," she confided in a low voice while Stan greeted a colleague, "but I thought this evening was worth it."

"I hope you didn't spend everything," Amanda whispered. "This is a fundraiser, you know."

"Your father's already written a huge check," her mother retorted. She glanced around as if she were looking for someone.

"Jill said she'd be late," Amanda said, following her glance toward the people filing into the ballroom. "The babysitter couldn't get there until after 8:00."

"Oh, I know, I know," her mother said absentmindedly. "I don't know where he could have gone to."

"Who?" Amanda asked.

"Why, Doug." Her mother turned around and frowned at her. "He walked in the door with us, and then he just disappeared."

Amanda suddenly felt very cold, even though the evening was warm, and hundreds of candles were burning in the room. "Doug's here?"

"Well, of course he is." Patricia peered at Amanda. "You *did* expect him to come, didn't you? He said he bought a ticket as soon as he heard about it."

Her mouth felt dry, and she licked her lips nervously. "I guess I just didn't think about it." She glanced around the room and breathed a sigh of relief when she didn't see him. "Mom, I need to check on things. You and Dad have a great time tonight."

She hurried across the room toward the kitchen, straining for the sight of a tall man with dark hair. *I can't see him tonight; I have too much to do,* she thought. *I don't need this. Why can't he just leave me alone?*

Megan caught her arm in front of the kitchen doors. "Amanda, what's the matter with you? You look like you're running away from a fire." She glanced around the room. "We've really attracted the crowd tonight. This should give the project a great start." She focused back on Amanda's face and frowned. "But you can't look like you've just lost your best friend. This is a party. Relax."

"Megan, I appreciate your help," Amanda said tightly. "But right now, I need to go into the kitchen."

"I don't think right now is a good time," Megan said softly, nodding gently over Amanda's shoulders.

Amanda knew before she turned around that Doug was standing there. She revolved as if in slow motion, and her breath caught in her throat when she saw him.

The tuxedo molded his tall body, accentuating his broad shoulders and narrow hips. His hair had been brushed until it glowed, and yet the unruly lock of hair still fell over his forehead. Just as she did in her dreams, she reached up and flicked it into place.

"Thank you," he said with a soft gleam in his dark eyes. "I never can get it to behave."

Megan had dissolved into the growing crowd. Amanda faced him, barely aware of the people around them.

"You've done a wonderful job." He glanced around the room before returning his dark gaze to her.

"I didn't do it alone. I had a lot of help."

"You organized it." A warm glow filled his eyes and he gave her his lopsided grin. "Don't be so modest, Amanda. You deserve the credit tonight. You've worked hard for this project."

She started to speak, and he lifted his hand. "And don't say it's just your job. You put your heart and soul into this effort."

No, she thought, amazed at the revelation, *you have my heart and soul.*

The words slammed against her heart, vibrating through every pore in her body. She couldn't ignore her feelings any longer. She loved him, she wanted to spend her life with him, to raise a family, to share their hopes and dreams.

This is Doug, she reminded herself. He's already had one love, one happy-ever-after. He doesn't want another one.

But surrounded by candles and bouquets of flowers, in the midst of beautifully gowned women escorted by handsome men in tuxedos, anything seemed possible.

Chapter Twelve

Her earlier fears about being with him vanished. For just this night, she would take what she was given. He was here, beside her. She would enjoy each moment and not worry about the future.

She smiled, letting her love for him shine in her expression. His grin faded. "Amanda, are you all right?"

"Of course." She fluttered her hand toward the ballroom. "Everything's going perfectly . . ." Her smile wavered for a moment at the memory of the mishmashed desserts before she rallied. "I'm just going to enjoy the evening."

"Then dance with me."

She wanted nothing more than to be held in his arms. But not in the middle of a dance floor. "I don't know how," she confided.

His eyes widened. "You don't know how to dance?" His skepticism showed in his voice. "You've never been to a dance before?"

"I've been to dances," she sputtered, wondering how she could be both exasperated and in love at the same time. "Just not with this kind of music."

The older guests dipped and swayed around the room, their bodies moving in perfect rhythm to the orchestra's big band sound. Doug watched them for a moment and then swung his attention back to Amanda. "Later, then," he said, and his words held a sultry promise.

She nodded, her hands clammy at the thought of being in his arms. *Tonight,* she thought, *tonight is my night. I deserve this one night at least.*

She didn't know what they talked about, only that she wanted the moment to go on forever. When a waiter stopped and asked her to go into the kitchen, she felt a strong desire to ask the young man to take care of the problem himself.

"I'm taking you from your duties," Doug said. "I'll see you later."

Before she could ask the waiter to find Megan, Doug strode off, his heels clicking authoritatively over the polished floor. As she slipped into the kitchen, she saw one of the doctors hail him, and he quickly became part of their laughing group.

Cindy stood by a tray of desserts, their misshapen bodies now an art deco design. "Amazing," Amanda said.

"Do you think they'll be all right?" The caterer adjusted the bow tie of one of the waiters holding a platter of shrimp puffs. "Don't drop them," she hissed.

The waiter gave his boss a jaunty grin and winked at Amanda. Cindy sighed. "The help you get nowadays."

"The desserts look wonderful," Amanda assured her, glad that this minor crisis had been averted. "I don't think anyone will know what happened."

"I hope so. I wanted this night to go perfectly."

Amanda knew Cindy hoped to drum up orders for her fledgling business. She assured her again that everything looked fine.

"Now if nothing else will go wrong, we should be okay." The caterer rearranged several finger sandwiches on a silver tray, her eyes darting toward another platter even as she worked.

Amanda backed toward the door. "I'll leave you. Just send someone after me if you need anything else."

Back in the ballroom, she spotted her sisters with their mother. She made her way in their direction, stopping to thank different people for coming and accepting the congratulations on both the vote's outcome and the dance.

"Let me see," Jill said when Amanda arrived next to them.

Amanda spun around, careful not to let the full skirt catch under anyone's feet. "You look beautiful," Christine breathed.

"I feel beautiful," Amanda confessed. "I can't imagine the difference a dress like this makes."

The emerald dress had cost more than she had ever paid for any of her clothes. Dressed and standing in front of her mirror, she knew it had been worth every penny. The scooped neckline set off the slender column of her neck and the long sleeves ended in points at her wrists, showing off her hands.

And the skirt. Nothing she had ever worn before felt so luxurious, so feminine. The yards of material rustled when she walked, the soft silk whispering against her legs. Instead of her long stride, she found herself walking with a slow, graceful step, almost gliding through the sea of people that she met.

"Are you going to give up those suits you wear?" Jill asked.

Amanda ran her hand over her skirt. "And wear this to the office every day? It would probably be hard to ride my bike."

"Just hike it over your shoulder," Christine offered.

They laughed at the picture of Amanda in emerald green silk riding her bike through town. Jill's face sobered first, and she clapped her hand around Amanda's arm. "What's *she* doing here?"

Amanda glanced around the room quickly, but she couldn't see anyone who would upset her sister. "Who?"

"Mrs. Carlson."

Amanda whipped her gaze back to Jill. "She's *here*?"

"She just came in."

Her height proved a blessing. Mrs. Carlson stood near the doorway, her petite frame draped in an elegant black gown. Her white hair was swept up, giving her the illusion of height. As Amanda watched, she gave a regal nod to the woman standing in front of her and then lifted her head to gaze directly into Amanda's eyes.

Amanda didn't flinch, forcing herself to meet that steely gaze. Mrs. Carlson gave a barely perceptible nod and then shifted her attention back to the couple she was with.

Jill's fingers bit into Amanda's arms. "You didn't invite her, did you?"

"Of course not. I suppose she bought a ticket like everyone else" Amanda disengaged her sister's hand and patted her fingers. "She won't cause a scene." *I won't let her,* she thought.

She edged her way through the crowd, this time barely able to accept the congratulations she was given. Once she neared Mrs. Carlson, the group around her shifted, and the two women found themselves face to face.

"Good evening." Amanda reached out a hand.

Mrs. Carlson's fingers were cold during the brief handshake. "Miss Blake." She surveyed the room and then smiled at Amanda. "You've outdone yourself, Miss Blake. A very impressive presentation."

Amanda inclined her head. "Thank you." She hesitated and then added, "I'm glad you were able to come tonight."

"I had little choice." The others had moved away, providing the two rivals with privacy.

"Oh?"

She gave Amanda a tight little smile. "You're too astute, Miss Blake, to play the surprised winner now. After your visit the other day, I realized that maybe you were right. I'm not saying that I was wrong. I tried to protect my daughters from the kind of children who will probably come to the community building, and now I was only protecting myself."

Amanda's eyes widened at this confession. "Oh, I'll deny it if you tell anyone else," Mrs. Carlson said. "I have a reputation to uphold as one of the community leaders. But I felt you at least deserved to know what happened."

"I suppose I should thank you for telling me."

"Someday, Miss Blake, when you have children, I hope you understand why I did what I did. I loved my daughters, Miss Blake, and I only wanted what was best for them."

Amanda saw the pain in the woman's eyes, and her heart softened a little. "You could still see your granddaughter as a princess. Rory said she wears the dress all of the time."

Mrs. Carlson chuckled. "Her mother used to do the same thing. She wore an old prom dress of mine until it practically fell apart."

She fixed Amanda with her commanding stare. "I may have accepted the fact that the community building will be in my neighborhood, but I intend to keep a close eye on their activities."

Amanda acknowledged the warning. "I think that's only wise, Mrs. Carlson. In fact, I'm sure they would appreciate your help." She spotted a familiar face and nodded toward an almost bald man standing in the midst of the doctors' group. "Do you know Dr. Peterson? He's working with a group of boys, and I understand he'll be part of the board of directors."

"Harris Peterson?" Mrs. Carlson sniffed. "Where is he? I hope they don't give him the chance to run the place.

Like a battleship under full steam, she sailed into the crowd and toward the good doctor. Amanda grinned, relieved that her own confrontation with the older woman had gone so smoothly. And Dr. Peterson wouldn't back down from her bluster.

A hand touched her shoulder, and she turned to see Doug in front of her. "Our dance, I believe."

"I told you I don't dance."

"You can dance this one." He wrapped his arm around her waist and caught her hand with his other hand. "All you have to do is follow me."

He propelled her onto the dance floor before she could utter a single word of protest. Intent on keeping her balance and matching her body to his movements, she didn't recognize the tune that was being played. Once she identified the popular love song, she raised startled eyes to his face and then dropped her lashes quickly at the warm expression she saw in them.

They circled the floor twice without speaking. Doug's arms held her close, and her feet followed his steps easily. Her heart thumped against her chest, and she was conscious of his cologne, the fresh-ironed scent of his shirt only inches away from her face and the hard muscles of his back under her hand.

When they rounded the main doors a third time, Doug chuckled.

She lifted her head. "What?"

"You could at least act like you're enjoying yourself."

I am, she thought. *I feel like Rory's granddaughter must feel. I'm a princess at a ball, and if I'm not careful, I'll wake up and be in my old rags once again.*

She shook her head at the fanciful thought. Fairy-tale heroines had always seemed a cowardly group to her. They were always running away just when things were getting exciting.

"Stay," she said softly.

Doug stared at her. "What did you say?"

"Stay. Don't leave Coppertown just because you don't want to work at the car dealership anymore."

His hand tightened on hers. "Amanda."

"I'm not asking for any promises, Doug. Just another chance. I won't run away this time."

"You were right, though. If I stayed, I'd only hurt you like I did Mary."

"I'm willing to take that risk, Doug." She smiled at her, letting her love shine through her eyes. "We have to take risks, Doug, or life isn't worth living."

She could see the answer in his eyes even if he wouldn't admit it. He cared about her, he wanted her. She couldn't let him go out of her life before he realized the truth himself.

"What would I do, Amanda?"

"You could practice medicine again."

He shook his head. "No, Amanda. That part of my life is over. I can't go back."

She accepted his decision. "All right. What else do you want to do?"

The music ended, and he guided her to a quiet alcove. A waiter passed with a tray of drinks, and Doug picked one up for each of them. "I don't know. That's just it. Nothing appeals to me anymore. I can't settle down." He drained his drink in one gulp and set the empty glass on a low table beside them. "You were right, you know. I haven't grown up yet."

She put her glass next to his and grabbed both of his hands in hers. "Doug, I was upset and hurt. We've both said some foolish things. That doesn't mean we can't start over, see what the future holds for us."

He stepped away from her touch. "Amanda, you want too much from me." She could see the torment in his eyes.

"I'm sorry. I shouldn't have come tonight, but I needed to see you one last time'.[ep   An uneasy feeling stirred in the pit of her stomach, and the finality of his words frightened her. "What do you mean, 'one last time'?"

"I've already accepted a job with a friend on the west coast. I leave tomorrow afternoon."

"But you can't! The month isn't over."

He bent down and kissed the tip of her nose. "I can't stay any longer." His words breathed across her skin.

She wanted to clutch him, to beg him not to go, but they were in the middle of a crowded room. The fairy tale had ended in a blinding flash, and there wouldn't be any happy ending. Hardly able to believe it was happening, she watched him walk across the room and out of her life.

Amanda punched the buttons on her calculator. "Okay, if we go with the radio spots and a print campaign, we should be able to meet their budget needs."

Bob wrote down several figures as she read them off. "Mr. Reynolds did want a television ad," he offered.

"He can't have one. Not for the budget he's given us." She studied the paper in front of her. "If he could increase the amount by even a small fraction, and we cut back on the other media, we could run one some evening, maybe during local news." She tapped her finger against the figures. "I don't think it's the best use of his money, but if he's set on a television ad, we can give it to him."

Bob nodded and closed his folder. "I'll tell him when we meet together tomorrow morning." The meeting over, he stood up and then paused, one palm resting on her desk. "Amanda, are you all right?"

"Hmmm?" She was already going over another account, trying to match their schedule with that of the camera crew.

"You haven't seemed yourself lately. I mean, your aura seems very deflated, almost flat."

She lifted her head and tucked a loose curl behind her ear. "Bob, I thought we agreed that the readings and auras would stay out of the office."

"I know, I know. But ever since the fundraising dance, you've been working yourself to the bone." He raised his hand and shook his head. "It's not just me, Amanda. Mark, Sierra, Megan, we've all noticed it. You hardly ever go home. You're working yourself too hard."

"It takes a lot of work to start a business," she stated in a dismissive tone.

Bob didn't budge. "You've been running this business for two years now, Amanda. We have enough accounts to keep us busy until the end of the year, and more are coming in all the time." He bent down and peered at her face. "It's more than just work."

"Bob, I appreciate your concern. I just want to keep our reputation for finishing quality work on time. That's all."

He didn't look convinced, but he finally left the room. Once he was gone, Amanda dropped all pretense of studying the account. She swiveled her chair around and stared out of the window.

Two months. At first she had expected him to call, to tell her that he couldn't go away. But not a word. She had ridden past the car dealership a week after the dance, almost hitting a parked car when she saw a tall man bent over a car. But the stranger who straightened up, a puzzled smile on his face, bore little resemblance to Doug. She had pedaled away as fast as she could, the ache growing inside of her.

Work didn't stop the gnawing pain, but it kept her too busy to dwell on it. She threw herself into her work, going home hours after the rest of the office staff left and arriving at the office shortly after the sun rose. The spring evenings gave way to the longer evenings of summer, and she often didn't get home until the first stars made an appearance.

She was tempted to stop and ask his cousin if he knew where Doug had gone, but the thought of exposing her feelings to anyone scared her. And what would she say? "Oh, by the way, Dick, do you know where Doug is? Yes, after just two weeks of knowing your cousin, I've fallen in love with him. But you know, he got away before I could find out where he was going."

She cringed at the imagined expression on Dick's face. The dance had given her a false sense of confidence. She had been so certain that once she declared herself, Doug would admit his own feelings.

"And what?" she muttered to herself now. "Live happily ever after? You should know better by now. You just have no luck when it comes to men."

She pushed Doug out of her mind and concentrated on the account in front of her.

When Megan buzzed her, she groped for the phone without tearing her attention away from the ideas she was sketching. "Yes, Megan?"

"Dr. Peterson just called. He wondered if you could come by the Willowton house this afternoon. He has something he wants to show you."

Amanda dropped her pencil on the desk. "The Willowton house?"

"Yes. He thought you'd be interested in their progress so far."

She hadn't been near the Willowton house since Doug's departure. Memories flooded her every time she thought of him, and even the file folder for the project reminded her of the touch of his arms around her.

"Amanda, you have to go out there," Megan said.

"Why? Our part of the project is over for now. Later, if they want some p.r. for the programs, then we can get involved again."

"They're saying you're afraid of Mrs. Carlson, that even though the vote was approved for the building, you don't want to confront her."

"You know that isn't true," Amanda said.

"I know it isn't, Amanda. But I've heard rumors."

Most people wouldn't believe rumors, but they could hurt her business. Rubbing a hand through her curls, she took a deep breath and released it slowly.

"So what do you suggest, Megan?"

"You need to work on the project. Or at least appear on a regular basis, take an interest in what's happening out there."

At the implied challenge in Megan's voice, Amanda sat up straighter. "All right. I'll go out tomorrow." She started to shift the phone away from her ear.

"No, today," Megan said. "You can't keep putting this off, Amanda. And Dr. Peterson wants you to come out today."

Resigned to the fact that she would get no work done with her secretary pestering her about the visit to Willowton house and Bob's worry about her "deflated aura," she sighed. "I'll go out today. When I get finished with this project."

"Now."

Amanda bristled at the single command and then relaxed. "Megan, I have to finish this report, and then I'll go. I *am* the boss," she finished softly.

Megan laughed. "All right, if it makes you feel better. But don't wait too long, or I'll escort you there myself."

Amanda hung up the phone and stared at the ideas that had fascinated her only minutes earlier. The newspaper contained details of the work being done at Willowton, and she had seen scattered news reports since the night of the fundraiser, but she did want to see the building for herself.

She grabbed her backpack and clicked off the office light. She had to face facts. Doug was gone, and she would have to go on without him. It was time to start moving forward again.

Chapter Thirteen

"I'm going now," she informed Megan as she passed through her office. "Is that acceptable?"

Megan surveyed her carefully. "Good, you need to get more fresh air." She leaned her elbows on the desk. "And don't worry about coming back today. I'll lock up the office."

The heat hit her with a blast when she walked out of the office building. A hot breeze whipped against her face, and she lowered her head, her legs pumping against it.

By the time she arrived at the Willowton house, her blouse clung to her skin. Beads of sweat trickled down her cheeks, and she wiped her hand against her face after she removed her helmet.

"You made it." Dr. Peterson hurried forward and tugged at her arm. "Come on, come on. I want to show you what we've done."

She draped the helmet over her bike and scurried after him. Several older women knelt by a flower bed at the right side of the steps, and a crew pounded new shingles on the roof.

A fresh coat of paint brightened the front of the building, and the loose boards of the porch had been nailed into place. The afternoon sun sparkled on shiny new windows.

Inside the house, she stepped around a man measuring curtains. "It looks wonderful," she enthused.

"The renovations are going quickly," Dr. Peterson agreed, leading her up the wide staircase. "But I wanted to show you something else."

He opened a door at the top of the stairs. A large wooden table and three file cabinets barely made a dent in the huge room. "Over here."

He picked up a ledger and flipped through the pages before jabbing his finger at the bottom of the page. "Look, Amanda, we did it!"

The large number blurred before her eyes. She studied it and then lifted her head, puzzled. "What is this?"

"The amount of money we've collected!"

At his crow of delight, she studied the amount again. "That much money has been donated for the project?"

He nodded, and her face broke into a grin. "We did it!"

He grabbed her arms and danced her around the room in a little jig. She tossed back her head, letting the sheer excitement of the moment wash over her.

"I see the old fool's given you the news, too."

Amanda stilled at the sound of Mrs. Carlson's voice. The older woman stood just inside the doorway, crisp in her gray linen suit.

Amanda brushed back her hair, aware that she was wilting in the afternoon heat. Even Mrs. Carlson's sarcasm couldn't stop her exalted feeling. And she could tell the older woman was having no effect on the man beside her.

"Come on, Ruth, you have to admit this is pretty exciting." Dr. Peterson mopped his perspiring face with a large handkerchief.

"At least I know the city won't be required to give any more funds toward the project."

Harris grinned at Amanda. "She's really excited about the project, but she's afraid to let anyone see it. Ruin her reputation, you know. And a smile could crack her face," he added in a stage whisper.

Amanda risked a quick peek at Mrs. Carlson. Her pressed lips still gave the impression of a woman barely tolerating a situation, but she thought she detected a slight twinkle in her eyes.

"I just came to tell you I've finalized my plans. I leave tomorrow, and I'll be gone for the next two weeks. But I'll expect a full accounting when I return."

"Of course. I always like to hear your ideas." He tipped his head toward Amanda. "Ruth, here, knows how to organize. She's keeping us on the straight and narrow, and saving time besides."

"Thank you." Again that softening in her eyes. "And I suppose I should thank you, Amanda."

Amanda swung her startled gaze to Mrs. Carlson. "Me?"

"I'm going to Seattle." One corner of her mouth curled up. "I've talked with Rory, and we're going to see if we can't settle our differences."

"Oh, that's wonderful, Mrs. Carlson."

"You could call me Ruth." At Amanda's quick gasp, the other corner curved in the semblance of a smile. "We are going to be working together."

Bemused, Amanda nodded. She watched from a corner of the room while Dr. Peterson went over some notes with Ruth.

Maybe she just needed something to fill her time, she thought. She had never met Mr. Carlson, only heard about the renowned international lawyer from others in town. He was often away on business, representing companies in a number of countries.

Her own mother had never worked outside the home, but her family, her church and community work all kept her busy. Amanda knew the different organizations relished Patricia's help, and her mother had never seemed to lack in self-esteem or purpose.

She studied Ruth Carlson more closely when the older woman bent over a drawing Dr. Peterson was showing her. She had quickly drawn together an opposition group when the inheritance was first announced. If Amanda hadn't been able to counteract her accusations, the vote could have gone the other way. Instead of standing on the second floor of a beehive of activity, they would be standing in the middle of a leveled piece of land.

"Amanda, what do you think?"

Amanda swung her attention back to the couple. "I'm sorry, I was thinking about everything that's happened."

Dr. Peterson grinned. "Great. But we were wondering about your opinion."

She stepped forward, glancing at the papers on the table. "On what?"

Dr. Peterson hitched up his pants leg and leaned against the table. "We're trying to find a director for the program. So far, none of the applicants have even come close."

Ruth tapped a stack of papers. "Most of them are young and haven't had much experience with people."

"Or with running any kind of organization," Dr. Peterson put in.

"But the board will be involved, won't they?" Amanda asked.

"Oh, we'll help with policies, procedure," Ruth said. "But we won't deal with the day-to-day running."

"We need someone who could run his or her own business." Dr. Peterson rubbed his hand over his chin. "And also knows how to work with people."

It would be a sacrifice, but she could survive without him. And how could she stand in the way of such a great opportunity? "I think Bob would be perfect," she admitted.

They both stared at her. "Bob?" Dr. Peterson asked.

Amanda gave them a puzzled look. "That is who you were thinking of, isn't it? Bob Owens, from my office? I've always thought he should run his own business, and this would be perfect for him."

"Bob." Dr. Peterson chuckled. From outside the room, Amanda heard shouts from the roofing crew just before a large pile of old shingles flew past the window.

"I don't think I know this man," Ruth said.

"Oh, you'd like him," Dr. Peterson stated before Amanda could say anything. "He's a hard worker and he's very organized." He slanted an amused glance toward Amanda. "Unless he's in the throes of one of his readings."

"Dr. Peterson!"

He grinned. "Well, you have to admit, Amanda, he has a different way of looking at the world. And I agree with Ruth. I think it's time you called me Harris."

She returned the grin, thinking of the fuss Bob had made that morning about her aura. "He does look at things from a unique perspective, *Harris*," she said, giving his name extra emphasis. "But he works hard," she argued.

"He does." Harris shifted and stood up. "No, we were thinking about someone who has successfully run a business already. Someone who needs a different direction and would be a welcome asset to the community."

"Who?"

She knew they were both watching her carefully, but she still wasn't prepared when Harris said simply, "Doug."

The room felt suddenly too hot. Her thoughts whirled around in her head, and she wondered if she was going to faint for the first time in her life. Doug was coming back to Coppertown?

"He sent in an application? But I thought you said you hadn't received any good ones."

Ruth nodded. "We haven't. But Doug's been working in Seattle with my son-in-law, and we thought my visit would be a good time to approach him."

Doug was in Seattle? Of course. His friend on the west coast. He must have met Rory's husband when they both lived in Coppertown.

"Amanda didn't flinch under Harris's steady gaze. "What makes you think he'll come back?" she asked.

"We don't know if he will. That's why we wanted your opinion," Harris said.

"I don't have any idea," she told them honestly. "I haven't heard from him since the fundraiser dance. And until just now, I didn't even know where he was."

Ruth gathered up several papers. "Well, then, we'll just have to see what he says." She was again her brisk self as she headed toward the door.

Her softer side returned when she paused in the doorway. "I'll do my best to persuade him." Her eyes met Amanda's in a woman-to-woman exchange.

"Thank you."

After she left, Harris showed her around the building. "This is where my boys will meet," he said proudly, ushering her into a wide open room in the back of the second floor.

He pointed out the many-shelved storage cabinet, the newly installed science counter, complete with sink, and several other amenities. She tried to respond appropriately, but he finally stopped his chatter with a rueful glance. "You don't really care, do you?"

She grasped his hands. "I *do* care. I'm still just a little stunned. I didn't think I'd ever see Doug again. The thought of him coming back to town . . ." Her words trailed off and she gave Harris a tiny smile.

He nodded and led her to the sofa placed under one of the windows. "I wanted to tell you earlier, but he asked me not to."

The familiar pang settled in the vicinity of her heart. "Is he happy?"

"No." He patted her hand. "And when I saw you today, I knew I couldn't let it go on."

"But what can I do?" She lifted anguished eyes to him. If only convincing Doug of her love was as easy as finding a new idea for one of her clients.

Her mouth dropped open. Of course!

Harris watched her closely. "What is it?"

She shifted around until she faced him. "I've been going about this all wrong. I thought my relationships and my business were separate, but they're not. My business is just another facet of who I am."

She thumped the arm of the couch. A gleam appeared in Harris's eyes. "So your new campaign is Doug?"

She grinned. "And you know how much I hate to lose."

She planted a kiss on the top of Harris's bald head and jumped to her feet. "I really do want to see the building, but I've got to get busy."

Harris bustled after her. "If Ruth can get him to come back and interview for the job, you'll have a perfect opportunity to play your hand."

Amanda stopped and Harris bumped into her. "I don't want him to take the director's job."

Harris frowned. "But if he doesn't take the director's job, what will he do?"

"Last year, Coppertown lost one of its premier doctors when he retired." He acknowledged her compliment with a grin. "My sisters are always complaining about the lack of good doctors for my niece and nephews. Doug was born to be a doctor. You know how upset his colleagues were when he left. And I know how involved he was in the community."

"He can be awfully stubborn," Harris warned her.

"So can I. Just ask my family."

Harris followed her down the steps. "Well, I hope you're successful. But that still won't get us a director. And without a director, the Willowton house won't survive."

She stepped onto the porch, fumbling in her backpack for her sunglasses. "You already have the perfect candidate," she informed him. "Ruth would be the perfect director."

She left him standing on the porch, his mouth open in surprise. With a wave, she hopped onto her bike and pedalled back into town.

Megan was just locking the door when she pushed her bike down the hall. "I told you not to come back."

"I know." Amanda propped the door open with her hip and slid the bike inside. "This is not about work, though, so you can go home and not worry about me."

Megan's eyes narrowed. "What is it then?"

Amanda hesitated. Her friend's help would be invaluable, and she didn't have much time. She'd wasted too much already.

"I'm starting a new project," she said. "Operation Dr. McCallister."

"Great! I wondered when you'd wake up." Megan pushed her way back into the office. "Come on, let's get busy."

Inside her office, Amanda yanked open her desk drawer and pulled out a newspaper clipping. She handed it to Megan. "What do you think?"

The picture was from the people section of the Sunday paper and had been taken at the fundraising dance. Doug held Amanda in his arms; their eyes smiled into each other's as they danced.

Megan whistled. "When I saw this picture, I thought you were the perfect couple. Several people commented on it while you were dancing." She handed the picture back to Amanda. "I couldn't believe he left."

"He doesn't want to be hurt again." Amanda rummaged in her desk and pulled out tablets, pens, and markers. She lined them up in front of her and grinned. "Okay, Megan, this is your chance to show me you're not just a secretary. What do we do now?"

For the next two hours, they scribbled and argued, adding notes to their tablets and sketches to their posters. Amanda made several phone calls before she finally leaned back in her chair and laced her fingers behind her head. "What do you think?"

"I think he doesn't stand a chance."

"That's what I'm counting on."

By the time their flight landed in Seattle the next morning, Amanda could hardly sit still. Ruth touched her hand. "Amanda, you need to get control of yourself. Think of this as just another campaign."

One that will affect my whole life, Amanda thought. She nodded, though, recognizing the wisdom of Ruth's words.

The taxi stopped in front of an attractive one-story house in a new development. As they waited for the driver to take out their luggage, Amanda realized that Ruth was now the anxious one.

She slipped an arm around the older woman's waist and gave her a quick squeeze. "It will be all right. She was thrilled that you were coming when I talked to her last night."

Ruth shut her eyes but not before a single tear slid down her cheek. "I just don't think I can bear it if things don't work out."

The door of the house opened. A woman a few years older than Amanda paused in the doorway. "Mother?"

Ruth took a tentative step forward. "Go on." Amanda gave her a push.

The two women met on the sidewalk, stopping inches apart. Then they were in each other's arms, laughing and crying and talking all at once.

The cab driver held the bags in his arms. "What do I do with these?"

Amanda plucked the bags out of his arms. "Here, I'll take them." She paid him and sat down on the bags, watching the tender scene in front of her.

"Oh, Amanda, I'm sorry, how rude." Ruth brushed at her cheeks and led her daughter toward Amanda. The introductions over, they carried the luggage into the house.

After being shown to her room, Amanda settled on the bed. She gnawed on her bottom lip, going over again every step of the campaign she had planned with Megan. *This has to work. If he goes away this time, I might never find him again.*

A knock sounded on the door. "Amanda?" Rory poked her head into the room at Amanda's call to come in. "I'm ready to go shopping."

By the time Rory's husband, Paul, arrived home from work, the plan was in full swing. Ruth's granddaughters had been shuttled to a neighbor's house with a promise to see Grandma all the next day. The three women were busy with the results of their shopping trip.

Paul leaned against the kitchen counter and folded his arms over his chest. "I almost feel sorry for Doug."

"Don't." His wife scooped up a picture in a plastic cover. "Look at this."

He studied the newspaper clipping of the dance and then glanced at Amanda. "He never talks about it, you know."

"That's good," Ruth said, opening a cupboard and pulling out dishes. She set the table with efficient movements, stepping back to study the effect before shifting a glass a fraction of an inch. "That means he still feels something."

Amanda hoped she was right and added the image to the others she had stored for support. Bob had returned to the office just before she left. He had beamed at her, thrilled by the change in her aura. The images would shore up her courage while she persuaded Doug how much they meant to each other.

A few minutes later, Ruth shooed them out of the kitchen. "We have to give Amanda time to get dressed," she said. "And we don't want to be here when Doug arrives."

Rory gave Amanda a quick peck on the cheek. "Good luck."

"Don't forget your strategy," Ruth cautioned her. She hesitated and then gave her an awkward hug before following her daughter and son-in-law out of the house.

Amanda took a steadying breath. She showered quickly, spending extra time on her makeup and hair. With shaking fingers, she unhooked her emerald dress from the hanger and slipped it over her head. Once she started dinner, she didn't want to leave the kitchen for even a minute and risk a repeat of her last cooking efforts.

Enveloped in a voluminous apron, she added rice to the chicken in the skillet. She turned on the timer and perched on the edge of a kitchen chair.

When it dinged, she carefully added the rest of the ingredients. She had just popped the lid back on when the doorbell rang.

Chapter Fourteen

She wiped her wet palms on the apron and tugged on the strings. Rolling it into a ball, she stuffed it into a cupboard and swallowed.

Her steps slow, she reviewed the plans she had made back in Coppertown. She grasped the doorknob, counted to ten, and swung it open.

Doug's startled gaze started her heart pounding under the silk of her gown. "Amanda?"

She nodded and waved him inside. "Hello, Doug."

He didn't move. "What are you doing here?"

"Fixing dinner." She held the door wider. "Would you like to come in?"

His eyes didn't leave her face as he walked into the house. She closed the door behind him and headed for the kitchen.

His fingers on her arm jerked her to a stop. She could feel their warmth through the filmy material and a desperate

174

ache crept upward. "What are you doing here?" he repeated.

"I'm fixing you dinner," she clarified. "The family took Ruth out to dinner."

"Ruth?"

"Mrs. Carlson, Rory's mother. We flew out here together."

Confusion spread across his features, and he rubbed both hands over his face. "You came out here with Mrs. Carlson, and you call her 'Ruth'?"

Amanda nodded, heading back toward the kitchen. This time he let her go. "Since we're going to be working together with the Willowton project, we thought it was foolish to stay enemies." She slowed down and added over her shoulder, "I think she's been looking for something to do since her daughters moved away. She sounds lonely."

Doug dropped into a chair. "I don't understand any of this. What are you doing here? How did you find me?"

"You didn't hide very well." She busied herself pouring drinks, careful not to spill on her unprotected dress. "Did you want to be found?"

He twitched and a shuttered look came into his eyes, shielding their expression from her. "It won't work, Amanda. I've already told you that."

She didn't say anything. She had been prepared for his arguments, but for just a moment, at the bleak nature of his words and his voice, misgiving swept through her.

She mentally stiffened her spine. The salads were already on the table, and she dug out the salad dressing from the refrigerator, keeping her back to him until she knew she had her emotions under control. "The first course is ready."

Her voice sounded unnaturally high, and she pitched it lower. "We can eat the salad while we wait for the paella to finish."

"Paella?"

She lifted her chin. "Yes."

One corner of his mouth quirked. Her chin lifted higher. "I'm trying to recreate a mood," she said in her haughtiest voice.

His lopsided grin came into full play. "Do Paul and Rory know what happened that night? I think they're rather attached to this house."

She resisted the urge to swing the bottle of salad dressing at his head and concentrated instead on his words. At least he doesn't seem like a man ready to bolt out the door, she thought, and her spirits lifted.

While they ate, she asked him questions about his new job, but his earlier mood had descended again. He answered with monosyllables, crunching lettuce and carrots in between questions. The sound grated on her nerves, and she jumped from her feet too quickly when the timer went off.

Her salad dish upended in her lap, sending pieces of lettuce across the wide skirt. Crushed, she stared at the stains slowly seeping into her beautiful dress.

"Let me help." Doug reached over and plucked off a bite of tomato and a piece of lettuce.

"No!" She batted his hand away, too embarrassed to look at him. Holding the skirt between her hands, she carried the scraps over to the sink and shook them off.

"I'll be right back." Her back still to him, she almost ran out of the kitchen and into her room.

She sank onto the edge of the bed, her fingers plucking at her skirt. When she felt a damp spot, she sighed and stood up, carefully pulling the dress over her head. She gently blotted the larger spots before tossing it on the bed, afraid that she would do more damage by trying to clean it then if she left it alone.

Clad in ivory slacks and a flower-patterned blouse, she went back into the kitchen. Doug was bent over the frying pan, the lid in his hand.

She rushed into the kitchen. "I didn't burn it again, did I?"

He swung around. "No, I turned it off when you left." He sniffed, putting the lid back on the pan. "It smells delicious. What else do you need to do?"

"Nothing. It's ready." She unplugged the pan and picked up the detachable serving dish. Doug placed a trivet in the center of the table for her.

He served them both. This time they ate in virtual silence. She had exhausted her list of questions, and he didn't seem inclined to carry his end of the conversation. *We can't talk to each other unless there's a crisis,* she thought. *I've got to do something, or we'll be finished, and he'll walk out the door.*

"How long have you known Paul?" she asked, desperate for a topic that couldn't be answered with a yes or no.

"Almost twenty years. We met when I visited my cousin. Then I moved into town, and we used to double-date before he married Rory." His voice broke off, and she knew he was thinking about Mary.

You have to do this, she told herself. *You have to bring Mary into the open.*

"Doug, do you remember when we met for lunch at the diner?"

He nodded, a wary look in his eyes. "You commented about my parents' marriage, that I was lucky to have such a loving relationship as an example." She took a deep breath and plunged on. "I feel the same way about Mary."

The shuttered look was coming back into his eyes. She couldn't let him pull away from her. Leaping to her feet, she ran around the table and knelt in front of him, grabbing his face with both hands and pulling his gaze back to her.

"Doug, I love you. And you love me. I can see it in your eyes." She released his face with one hand and reached around for the picture from the newspaper. She thrust it under his nose. "Look at this. Can you deny that you care about me?"

He blinked, and she moved the picture away, so that he could focus on it. He studied the picture before meeting her eyes. "Amanda, this doesn't change anything."

"Yes, it does. If you love me, how can you run away?" An appalling thought flashed into her mind, and she rocked back on her heels. "Is that why you keep running away? Have you left women all over the country?"

His hands gripped her shoulders. "No! Since Mary, I wasn't able to look at another woman until you came into the dealership."

She caressed his cheek with the back of her hand. "Doug, Mary loved you. She wouldn't want you to be so unhappy. And for what? You can't run away from every risk there is in the world. You have to take chances."

His hands gentled and his fingertips stroked her shoulders. She tipped her head, resting her cheek on his hand. One finger lightly rubbed her cheek.

They stayed that way for several minutes, but she couldn't stop halfway.

"Doug, Harris told me that you're still licensed as a doctor in Missouri."

His hand froze against her skin. "And?"

The chilly tone almost deterred her, but she had to banish that futile look in his eyes. "And Coppertown needs another pediatrician. Since Harris retired, they haven't been able to find one willing to locate in town."

"I'm not practicing again."

She sighed, wondering how many times they would clash. This time, she was determined to win. "Then why did you keep taking the required courses? Why did you keep paying the yearly fees? If you didn't want to be a doctor anymore, why didn't you let your license lapse?"

"You *are* stubborn, aren't you?"

His words stung. "Yes," she snapped. "And I can hold out for a lot longer than you can." *I'm fighting for our future,* she thought.

She clutched his hands, her heart throbbing against her ribs. "Doug, if you turn your back on your medicine, on love, you're turning your back on Mary and everything she stood for. Is that the way you want to remember her?"

A ragged cry edged over his lips. "Amanda, this isn't fair."

Her tone softened. "Life isn't fair, Doug. But we can't give up." Her hand smoothed back the hair over his forehead. "We need each other, Doug. You've shown me that I don't have to be alone, that I can depend on someone without losing my own person."

His fingers rubbed against the sensitive skin of her wrist. "And I think you need me," she whispered, "to remind you that love is more powerful than any pain we ever feel."

"You are stubborn, aren't you?" he repeated, but this time the words were encased in love.

She leaned her forehead against his. "I think it's only fair to warn you, you're my latest campaign. And I can be pretty determined."

His bark of laughter echoed throughout the room just before he gathered her into his arms.

Somehow, she found herself sitting on his lap, her arms wrapped around his neck. "It's not going to be easy," he said, his words muffled against her skin as he peppered a trail of kisses from her lips to her eyelids and back again.

"I know." Her hands buried themselves in his thick hair, liking the springy feel of it under her fingers.

"I'll get phone calls at all hours."

"You'll have to eat my cooking," she countered.

He lifted his head, an arrested look in his eyes. "I never thought of that. Here I was thinking you were the one making all of the sacrifices. . . ."

She effectively stopped his words with a kiss. When their lips separated, her head rested on his shoulder while his hand caressed her back.

"I don't think I can be just a doctor's wife," she murmured in a tight voice. "I want to keep my business."

He tipped her chin up with one finger. "Amanda, I would never ask you to give up your business. We don't have to follow some already written script. We'll work it out together as we go along."

Her mouth dropped open. "What is it?" he asked.

"I just realized, we're talking as if we're going to be married, and you haven't even asked me."

He grinned. "Me? But this is *your* campaign, remember?"

She nodded, and he brushed her lips with a quick kiss, swallowing her words. "No, I don't think I want you to have that pleasure." With his hands on either side of her face, his dark gaze bored into hers, and she gave a delicious little shiver.

"Amanda Blake, I love you. Will you marry me?

"Yes," she answered, all her love radiating outward.

His head lowered. Just as his lips pressed against hers, she thought she heard a tiny, satisfying click. She smiled against his mouth. Her soul was now complete.

Epilogue

Amanda tapped on the pane of glass separating the waiting room from the receptionist's area. A little boy coughed behind her, and she gave him a sympathetic look before smiling at the young woman who opened the window.

"Oh, no, this doesn't mean you're taking our baby away?"

Amanda grinned. "*Our* baby? Is there something I should know about?"

The woman laughed. "She's such a doll. We've been fighting over who gets to watch her when he has a patient."

"Then I better take her home. Doug won't be happy if she's causing a ruckus in his office."

"Not happy with that little jewel in his office?" The receptionist shook her head and opened the inner office door. "I've never seen the doctor happier. He may be the one you have to fight to take her home."

Amanda chuckled and walked down the hallway toward a closed office door. She ran her fingers over the letters on the door proclaiming: DR. DOUGLAS McCALLISTER. Inside the office, she paused and grinned. Amidst the normal office clutter, a bassinet, complete with a hanging toy rail, sat in the far corner. Several stuffed animals, too big for the occupant of the bassinet, took up space on the desk and chairs.

She flung her purse into the middle of the desk and scooped up the tiny baby lying there. "Hello, precious." She rubbed her nose against her daughter's soft cheek.

"Hey, what do you think you're doing?"

She whirled around and grinned at her husband. "Come to claim my daughter. I understand she's been adopted by the entire office staff." She gestured around the empty room. "But where were her nannies just now?"

Doug shut the door and crossed the room in two quick strides. His right arm wrapped around her shoulders while he handed the baby the bottle with his left. "I just left her for a minute to get a bottle."

The baby clutched the bottle with both hands and slurped in loud gulps, her brown eyes, so like her father's, never leaving the source of her nourishment. While his daughter ate, Doug kissed Amanda's cheek and squeezed her tighter. The action brought an impassioned wail from their daughter.

"I don't think Kelsie's very interested in our relationship right now." He stepped away from Amanda and, after moving a particularly large gray bear, sat down in his office chair. "I'm glad you're home. I've missed you."

Amanda perched on a corner of his desk, the baby resting against her hip. The sounds of her eating filled the small room.

"I missed you, too," Amanda said finally, drawing her gaze away from the sight of her daughter. She smiled at Doug, amazed again at how much this man meant to her.

"Well, you're home now." He reached out a hand and touched her arm just above Kelsie's chubby little leg. "How was the conference?"

"Good. We made several important contacts, and Mark found a computer system that he really likes. Once he hooks it up, I don't even have to go to the office."

"You don't have to stay at home," Doug said gently.

"I know." She shifted Kelsie, so the baby could finish the last of her formula. "But a lot of what I do is paperwork. No reason I can't do it at home." She nuzzled Kelsie's forehead. The baby lifted one eyebrow but didn't stop drinking. "I'm not giving up my job. Just adapting my hours a little."

Doug stood up and pulled her toward him. The bottle, its purpose complete, slipped from the baby's mouth and slid to the floor. Cuddled between her mother and father, its owner didn't mind, only cooed and gurgled while her parents kissed above her head.